Delay

I0632415

How Do You Spell g·e·e·k?

by Julie Anne Peters

SCHOLASTIC INC.
New York Toronto London Auckland
Sydney Mexico City New Delhi Hong Kong

To my mother,
Kossuth County, Iowa, spelling champ of 1938

This edition published by arrangement with Little, Brown and Company,
New York, New York, USA. All rights reserved.

The characters and events portrayed in this book are fictitious. Any
similarity to real persons, living or dead, is coincidental and not
intended by the author.

No part of this publication may be reproduced, stored in a retrieval
system, or transmitted in any form or by any means, electronic,
mechanical, photocopying, recording, or otherwise, without written
permission of the publisher. For information regarding permission, write
to Little, Brown Books for Young Readers, a division of Hachette Book
Group, Inc., 237 Park Avenue, 15th Floor, New York, NY 10017.

ISBN 978-0-545-32251-5

Copyright © 1996 by Julie Anne Peters. All rights reserved. Published
by Scholastic Inc., 557 Broadway, New York, NY 10012, by arrangement
with Little, Brown Books for Young Readers, a division of Hachette Book
Group, Inc. SCHOLASTIC and associated logos are trademarks and/or
registered trademarks of Scholastic Inc.

12 11 10 9 8 7 6 5 4 3 2   11 12 13 14 15/0

Printed in the U.S.A.   40

First Scholastic printing, December 2010

How Do You Spell g·e·e·k?

1

Fwap. A thick book dropped onto the cafeteria table, rattling my tray.

I glanced up. "What's this?"

My best friend, Kimberly Tyne, said, "*Merriam Webster's Collegiate Dictionary,* tenth edition."

"I know what it is. What's it doing here?" I bit into my cheeseburger and added in a garble, "Ruining my lunch?"

Kimberly hooked a strand of straight blond hair over her right ear. "My mother started me on a schedule. If I don't practice every day, I won't make it through the rest of the alphabet by April."

My chin hit the floor. "Kimberly, we just finished the big area spelling bee on Friday. You won first place! Can't you even take a break?"

"I had a whole weekend off." She crossed her eyes at me. Pushing her oval designer glasses back up her nose, she eyed the dwindling buffet line. "Be back in a minute. You want anything?"

This stupid dictionary out of my sight, I thought. I shook my head.

Kimberly pointed to *Webster's*. "We stopped at the *M*'s, I think."

Gag. I jammed the cheeseburger into my mouth. We'd been spelling day and night since Thanksgiving to prepare for the Denver west area spelling bee. Ever since third grade, Kimberly and I had been spelling together, and getting farther every year. Eighth grade, this year, was our last time to compete. We shared a dream — to make it to the National Spelling Bee in Washington, D.C.

I was a good speller, but Kimberly was awesome. Last year she aced the county spelling bee, the first person ever to get every word right on the written test. I missed six. Even though it got me to the orals, Kimberly outlasted me there, too. She wound up placing third in the whole state of Colorado, while I came in a dismal twenty-third. But who's counting?

Kimberly slid into her seat with her tray. Squeezing open the wedge on her chocolate milk, she said, "How could you have missed *fuchsia*? It's your favorite color."

I choked, remembering what I was trying to forget

about last Friday's fiasco. "I don't remember ever seeing it written down." I'm a visual speller, which means I'm a lousy guesser on words I've never seen. Kimberly knows all the rules, variations, derivations. "So what?" I shrugged. "I still got third place. Still get to go to county."

"Bet you never forget *fuchsia*." Kimberly aimed her pizza at her mouth and flipped open the dictionary.

That's the truth. Once you misspell a word, you never forget it. "Doesn't matter." I swirled a stale French fry through a glob of ketchup. "I'm switching favorite colors." Wiggling the limp, gooey fry in front of her face, I said, "To red. R-e-d."

She laughed and passed the dictionary across the table. "First word."

Here we go again. I sighed wearily. "*Malacostracan*. Mal-uh-KOS-tri-kan. Derivation Greek." I sucked in a smile. Kimberly hates foreign words.

"Definition," she said.

I scanned the dictionary page to find the word again. " 'Any of a large subclass of crustaceans having a thorax consisting of eight segments usually covered by a carapace and including the decapods and isopods.' Yikes! Sounds like attack of the pod people."

"Crustaceans aren't people," she replied dryly. "They're like crabs."

I looked again. "Could be crabby pod people."

No response.

I picked up my milk and took a swig. "Okay. Here's a sentence. Did you sample the malacostracan salad last week? It was delectable, except the decapod shells got stuck in my teeth and I crunched all during study hall."

Something resembling a smile flickered across Kimberly's lips. A long moment passed. Then another. My hand waved in front of her eyes. "Yo, anybody home?"

"I'm thinking. *Malacostracan.* M-a-l-a . . ." She paused to push her glasses up her nose. "M-a-l-a . . . Did you say Greek?"

An audible sigh betrayed my impatience.

"Okay, okay. M-a-l-a-k-o-s-t-r-a-c-a-n."

"Errrrrt." My loudest buzzer imitation.

"I knew it. *C*, right? M-a-l-a-*c*?"

"I'm keeping score. So far it's Kimberly Tyne minus one, Ann Keller, zip. Hey, I'm ahead." For the first time ever.

She exploded. "You don't have to make a big deal out of every word I miss. I feel stupid enough as it is."

Then I exploded. "Stupid? When did you ever feel stupid? Every year we practice for the spelling bee, you start up where we left off last year. I have to relearn every word from *aardvark* on. Don't talk to me about feeling stupid." My voice shook. Even oblivious Kimberly noticed.

She lowered her eyes. "I'm sorry, Ann. I'm just under a lot of pressure. This is our last chance, and I really want to win. Everyone *expects* me to win. Especially you-know-who."

I knew who. Her parents. The little Hitlers. They expected Kimberly to be perfect. The one time she brought home a B on her report card, she had to do extra credit for the class.

"Well, tell your mom to stop worrying. You're not going to win the spelling bee this year."

She arched an eyebrow.

"That's right. I am. In fact, I'm going to Washington and I'm going to win there, too. So there." I stuck out my tongue.

Her eyes fixed on me. "You sound like you mean it."

"Just try to stop me."

The air between us suddenly chilled as we tried to intimidate each other with frozen stares. Naturally I blinked first. That was my problem — no killer instinct.

"Next?" I passed the dictionary back to her.

She studied the page. "This word is perfect for you, Ann," she said. "*Maladjusted*. 'Poorly or inadequately adjusted; specifically: lacking harmony with one's environment from failure to adjust one's desires to the conditions of one's life.' " She smirked.

"What does *that* mean?"

"Sentence: Ann Keller is severely maladjusted if she thinks she can beat me to the National Spelling Bee."

I sneered.

The warning bell jolted us back to reality. Hastily we

shoveled the remainder of our lunches into our mouths and scrambled for the cafeteria doors.

"Are we on tonight at your house?" Kimberly asked as she bounded gazelle-like down the hall.

"No, Dad has to work late again, and Chase is going to be home." I made an ugly face that only a brother could love. "Let's make it your place, six-thirty."

Kimberly waved over her shoulder while I slammed my locker in unison with — as usual — the late bell.

2

Study hall. A whole hour of pretending to do algebra while sneaking a peek ahead in my *Webster's*. Okay, I admit it: I'm a glutton for punishment. "*Maladjusted*," I mumbled. "M-a-l-a-d-j-u-s-t-e-d." I checked, just to be sure. What was the definition?

"Failure to adjust one's desires to the conditions of one's life." A sigh escaped my lips.

Kimberly was right. I was maladjusted. Definitely kidding myself about my chances this year. Everyone knew she'd win. She was the best. Plus, last year's first and second place winners had graduated to the ninth grade, leaving Kimberly alone at the top.

I glanced at the next word. *Meager.* Why wasn't it spelled m-e-e-g-e-r? Long *e*, right? *Medal.* Was it *medal*, *meddle, metal,* or *mettle?* You'd need bionic ears to hear the difference. Dad teased me once that Ann was short for Analyze.

The next word was a doozie. *Mnemosyne.* Ni-MOSS-en-ee — I stumbled over the pronunciation. The Greek goddess of memory. Good. I'd pray to her for help tonight — if I remembered.

Sick of practicing, I slammed the dictionary closed. Mr. Howell shushed me from the front of the room and got an apologetic shrug in response. Opening my algebra book, I took up my usual study hall position, head on arms on book. Staring out the window, where a Colorado spring snowstorm littered the air with frozen confetti, I repeated the *maladjusted* definition to myself. Lacking harmony with one's environment.

That hit home. My entire life was off-key. My parents' divorce was the pits. Dad kept the house since his computer consulting business was just a couple of miles away, and part of the time he worked in his office at home. Mom moved to Colorado Springs to open Keller Real Estate. She asked us to move with her, but Chase and I didn't really want to change schools. I mean, we grew up in Denver. All my friends were here. We saw Mom on weekends, when she wasn't busy, which was once a month, maybe, if we made an appointment. I missed her.

"Look, Annie, it's not that bad," my big brother Chase's voice echoed in my head. "We get two of everything now.

Two homes, two allowances, two working parents. If we play our cards right, we can really rake in the big ticket items — cars, CDs, computers. We just make sure Mom and Dad have to compete for us." His dark eyes twinkled mischievously.

What a material boy. Though maybe he was right. I could use a whole new wardrobe. Plus, if I had pair of leather boots, like the red Georgios Jennifer Caldwell was wearing beside me . . .

"Ann? Ann!" I blinked back to earth. Mr. Howell loomed over me, breathing onions from lunch on my face. "Mrs. Welter would like to see you in her office," he said.

"Why?" I shot upright. "I've only been late twice this week."

"Maybe you're receiving the high productivity study hall award." He chuckled as he handed me a hall pass. Adults were so terribly u-n-a-m-u-s-i-n-g.

The principal's office was filled with a lower-life assortment of middle school dropouts. Vacant-eyed flunkies hung around in the waiting area, straddling the wooden benches or just sniveling in place.

"I have a message from Mrs. Welter," I said, handing the school secretary my pink slip.

"Have a seat and I'll let her know you're here." She motioned me to park myself on a bench.

Considering all the diseases communicable through wood, I decided to stand. Not to appear totally stuck-up, I leaned against the wall and faked gum chewing. There was a geeky girl standing next to me. She smiled.

Revolting. A hunk of bread stuck in her braces.

Mrs. Welter's door opened suddenly. "The next time I catch you with cigarettes, it's an automatic suspension," she warned the turf-head leaving her office. "Do you understand, Dwayne?"

He mumbled some obscenity under his breath.

"Dwayne!"

He turned to holler, "Yeah!" and bumped into me. Cooties crawled up my arms. Clucking with disgust, I brushed off the invisible vermin.

"Oh, Ann, hello." Mrs. Welter caught me in her crosshairs. "Please come in." She motioned me into her office, which looked as if it had been bombed by terrorists in training. "Excuse the mess," she said, gesturing to a chair. "I was just reorganizing my files."

She took up her place behind the desk. Smiling at me through steel gray eyes she said, "I'd like to ask a favor of you."

I hate it when adults say that, like you get a choice.

"We have a new student starting today, and I thought it'd be nice if she had someone to show her around. You know, teach her about the way things are done here. Be her sponsor."

Inwardly I moaned. "Is she an exchange student or something?"

"No."

Then why would she need a sponsor? "She's not . . ." Oh, no, special ed?

Mrs. Welter said, "She's been home schooled all her life. I won't know where to place her until she takes her achievement tests. She comes from a small town in"— Mrs. Welter opened a folder —"Kansas, I think." She closed that folder, then opened another. "Or Nebraska."

Great. A hick. When was I going to have time to tutor a hick from the sticks? "Mrs. Welter, I appreciate your picking me, but I don't have time to tutor. My schedule is like totally full. Maybe Kimberly —" Oops, she wouldn't appreciate me dropping her name.

"I specifically chose you because this new girl's parents recently got divorced. I thought maybe you could use someone to talk to. Someone who's going through a similar experience." She cocked her head at me. "How are you coping anyway, Ann?"

"Swell," I mumbled. For some reason my eyes teared up.

Mrs. Welter went on, "You won't have to tutor. She just needs someone to show her the ropes, make her feel comfortable here at Shiffley. Since she's never been to public school, she might need a bit of catching up socially."

"Then the person you *really* want is Jennifer Caldwell," I said. "Now, she —"

Mrs. Welter cut me off. She leaned forward on her elbows, boring into my eyes. "If you're feeling overwhelmed, Ann, maybe I could arrange some counseling —"

"No!" Then everyone in school would know I was maladjusted. "I mean, it's not that. I-I guess I could show her around, if that's all it is."

"Wonderful. Are you ready to meet Lurlene?" Mrs. Welter stood.

Lurlene? What was she, a country-western singer or something? Introducing Lurlene Rae Jean from Aberdeen.

"She seems outgoing. You two should hit it off." The principal walked past me to the waiting room.

When they returned, I stood up. It was a natural reaction, since the only way out now was to dive through Mrs. Welter's window. Lurlene was that creepy creature with the braces I'd leaned next to in the waiting area.

"Ann Keller, meet Lurlene Brueggemeyer."

Lurlene flashed a mouthful of metal at me. "Hi again," she said.

Her ghastly appearance made me shudder. Frizzy pigtails festooned out of both sides of her head, secured by red rubber bands. I mean, they weren't even braids. To keep her bangs back, she had three or four pink bow barrettes scraping her skull. Puh-leaze.

As my eyes moved downward, the horror show got hairier. She was wearing . . . a jumper? A corduroy jumper over a-a checkered flannel long-sleeved shirt? Okay, maybe she was making a fashion statement — something like "back to the woods." But not . . . oh, no! She had on cowboy boots. Yeehaw.

"Ann will be your sponsor, Lurlene." Mrs. Welter's voice cut off my gawk. "She's one of our most outstanding students. And very popular." She winked at me. My face sizzled with humiliation. Or was that dread?

Lurlene turned to me. "Um, thanks," she said shyly.

I mumbled something I didn't really mean like, "No problem."

Mrs. Welter rummaged around in the paper jungle on her desk. "Here's your schedule." She handed Lurlene a list. "Your classes may change after I get your test results. Ann will show you to your locker and help you find your classrooms. Is there anything else?"

We both shrugged.

I paused outside the office door so that I could study Lurlene's schedule — and plot my escape. Lurlene said to me, "Mrs. Welter's really nice."

Without looking up, I replied, "Yeah, a lobotomy'll do that for you. She escaped from the mental ward a few months ago."

"What?"

I looked at Lurlene.

"Oh, you're kidding." She grinned. "That's funny."

I didn't reply. I was busy stifling disgust. Lurlene's schedule was unbelievable. She was in all the Level 1 classes — you know, for the "challenged" students. We had names for those classes: Human Experiments in Science, Reading Rainbow, Teen Skills for the Criminally Inclined.

"You weren't exactly home schooled at Harvard, were you?" I said.

Lurlene blushed. "I wish." She didn't say anything more, which stalled the conversation. But they don't call me rrr-Ann Off At The Mouth for nothing.

"Mrs. Welter said you moved here from Kansas or Nebraska."

"South Dakota," Lurlene corrected.

"Ah. So, you must know Laura Ingalls personally."

Lurlene laughed. She had a really loud laugh, and it drew attention to us.

I ducked my head. "Look, we'd better get to your locker and find your classroom or you're going to be late. You don't want to miss"— I glanced down at her schedule and mumbled, "Math for the Mental Giant."

3

Dad wasn't going to be home by the time I had to leave for Kimberly's, so I stuck a note on the fridge. "Dad — I made your dinner. It's in the freezer in that box that says 'Budget Gourmet.' Nuke and puke. I'll be home around nine. Your darling daughter."

Chase was home. He slammed the phone down just as I opened a can of Franco-American Spaghettios. On his way past, he grabbed the can.

"Hey, dog breath. Give it back. That's my dinner."

"Grrr," he growled. He yanked open the silverware drawer, saw it was empty, and unlatched the dishwasher. "These clean?" he said.

"How should I know? It's your week for KP."

Chase held a spoon up to the light. "No crusties." He

handed it to me and selected another for himself. Just to be safe, I rinsed mine off.

We sat at the breakfast bar, feasting from the can.

"You're in a mood," I said to Chase. "What happened? Sherilyn dump you? Or is it Nicole this week? I can't keep track."

He sneered at me. For a minute he didn't speak. Finally he swallowed his mouthful of Spaghettios and said, "I asked Mom to come to my wrestling meet on Saturday. It's the first round of semifinals, and she hasn't been to one meet all year. I thought she'd want to come see me pin my guy at least *once*." His lips tightened so hard, his dimples dented his cheeks.

This was Chase's first year wrestling, since he bombed out of every other sport in high school. Chase was short, like me, and kind of puny. Which worked to his advantage as a lightweight wrestler, he discovered with a vengeance.

"Mom have to work?"

"Nooooo." Chase made a face. "She wanted to know if Dad was going to be there. When I said, 'Yeah, probably, he usually comes,' she made up some lame excuse. A seminar on creative home financing or something."

Typical. Chase and I both shook our heads. "You know," I said, "when I asked her to come to the spelling bee on Friday, she said she couldn't make it either."

Chase looked at me. "She thought Dad was going to go?"

I nodded. From his expression, I could tell he hated this silent treatment between our parents as much as I did. It was almost worse than the screaming and door slamming. Almost.

We ate the rest of the can in silence. Then Chase slugged me in the shoulder and said, "Maybe we could exchange them for better models. That's it. We'll start this new service. The Parent Exchange. Hey, kids." He jumped to his feet and held his spoon to his mouth. "Get your parents here. Fully functional families. Lifetime guarantee. Call now. Operators standing by."

I snorted. Checking my watch, I said, "I gotta go. What time's the wrestling meet?"

"Four," he answered.

"Even if Dad can't come, Kimberly and I'll be there."

"Big thrill."

He didn't mean it. I knew he cared. As he chucked the empty Spaghettios can in the trash, I said, "Will you give me a ride over to Kimberly's?"

"I'm not your chauffeur." He swaggered across the living room and looped a leg over his workout bench.

"Turd." I kicked him hard on the way past.

It was frigid outside, at least a hundred below. By the time I got to Kimberly's, I was the human icicle. Mrs. Tyne answered the door. "Oh, hello, Ann. Come in. How are you, dear?" She gave me that look — you know, child of divorce? Abandoned kitten?

"Fine," I said, breathing on my fingers to thaw them. "Kimberly in her room?"

"Yes."

I made my escape by bounding up the stairs. "Ong-ko-ser-KY-uh-sus," Kimberly said before I even had the door closed. "*Onchocerciasis.*"

I flopped on the bed. "Parents." My loud exhale spelled unadulterated annoyance.

"Definition," Kimberly continued. " 'Infestation with or disease caused by filarial worms . . .' "

I wrinkled my nose. "Please, I just ate what looked like a can of worms."

Kimberly glanced at me over her glasses. "Are you going to spell or waste time pretending to be funny?"

"Excuuuuuuse me. O-n-c-h-o-s-e-r-c-i-a-s-i-s."

"Wrong," she said.

"Don't yell at me."

She blinked, her long eyelashes magnified through the thick lens of her glasses. "Sorry, Ann. But I'm not even halfway through the *O's*, and I have to finish the *R's* by Friday."

"Says who?"

She widened her eyes at me.

"Like I said, parents!"

Kimberly set the dictionary in her lap. "You and your mom have another fight?"

"No. It's just . . ." I lay back and stared at the ceiling. "I don't know. Everything's changed so much this year. Now Mom and Dad are avoiding each other at all costs, including Chase and me." I paused. "How can two people who used to be in love end up hating each other?"

Kimberly folded her arms over the back of her desk chair. "You got me. I'm never getting married. Or if I do, I'm not having kids."

"At least your parents support you. At least they know you're alive."

"Sometimes I wish they didn't. Sometimes I wish . . ." She blinked. Hefting the dictionary up, she said, "Do you mind?"

I sighed and sat up. "Let me write down that worm word in my spelling notebook." As I reached into my backpack to retrieve my dictionary and notebook, something struck me. "I thought we were at the *MA*'s at lunch. How'd we get to *O*?"

Kimberly mumbled, "My parents and I worked after school and a little during dinner."

It ticked me off that she'd go ahead without me, but I didn't say anything. As I opened my spelling notebook, a handwritten list fell to the bed. Lurlene's schedule. "Kimberly, you won't *believe* what I have to do. Mrs. Welter is making me show this geek around the school."

Kimberly's lips were moving, her eyes closed.

I continued, assuming her ears were tuned in. "She picked me because I'm such an outstanding student, and sooooo popular."

No response.

"Kimberly, that was a joke. You should see this girl. She's hideous. She has pigtails and wears barrettes and cowboy boots. The ones with pointy toes?"

That got Kimberly's attention. She zoned in. "You're kidding. Who is she?"

I launched into a detailed description. Just as I began reciting Lurlene's schedule from memory, a knock sounded on the door. We both jumped. The door opened a crack, and Mrs. Tyne poked her head in. "It's getting late, Ann. Time for Kimberly to get ready for bed." She opened the door all the way and came in. "So, how far'd you get?" Mrs. Tyne wandered over to the desk with a stack of folded clothes. Setting them down on the bureau, she glanced over into Kimberly's lap. "You're still in the *O's?"

Kimberly gave me a scary look.

All I could think was, Uh-oh.

*   *   *

I met Lurlene in the front office before school the next morning. It was her idea, not mine. She was wearing the exact same outfit as yesterday. No, wait — a striped shirt under the shift instead of the checks. Plus, she had on red kneesocks that were pulled up over the edges of her boots, then cuffed. No joke.

She must have heard me groan, because her eyes followed mine. "Anything wrong?"

"Uh, no. Nice boots." I felt a little ashamed for being so obvious.

"Thanks," she said. "They're Tony Lamas. I got them for Christmas."

Give them back, I almost blurted. "Come on, Lurlene," I said instead. "Let's find your first class. Do you need to stop at your locker?"

"No," she said. "Not really."

That's when I noticed she wasn't carrying anything. "Don't you have a notebook or something?" Keys, makeup, brush, comb, a curling iron — the bare necessities?

"Will I need one?" she asked.

"Unless you plan to carve notes into your desk. Here." I rummaged around in my book bag. "You can use my spelling notebook." It wasn't doing me much good copying down the words I missed, since I never looked at them again. "And here's a pencil." I handed her both.

"Thanks, Ann." She smiled metallically at me.

The hallways were empty as we started for her locker. I couldn't chance it, though. I hurried to stay at least two steps ahead.

"This is so different." Lurlene's voice filled the void between us. "So many people. And teachers. I never had more than one teacher." She glanced toward the gym, where an early morning faculty volleyball game was in progress.

"So, did you have P.E. in home school?" I asked. Stupid question. How could she have P.E. at home?

"Sort of," she said. "My brothers and I played baseball and soccer. We took hikes, stuff like that, when we were still a family." Her voice fell. I turned and noticed her face had deflated as well. Suddenly she brightened and said, "One time, I remember, Cal Larson's bull got loose, and we had to chase it down. It ran for six miles, right into the town dump. That bull was really mean, maybe even insane, and it kept charging us. My brothers and I had to defend ourselves with fence pickets and broomsticks until Cal finally coaxed the bull into his pickup. We were exhausted. My father said it counted for our week's quota of exercise. He called it a good game of 'bull hockey.'" She laughed.

I almost laughed, too, but then my worst nightmare materialized.

"Hey, Keller. You coming to the basketball game tonight?" Brad McKenzie grabbed my arm and spun me around.

I stared up into his incredible sky blue eyes. "I, uh, dunno. I might have other plans."

"Don't tell me. Spelling, right? You're such a nerd."

The titter behind me caught his attention. Brad peered over my shoulder, and I watched as his eyes filled with disbelief. Or horror. "Who, or what, is that?" he whispered.

I pushed him backward a few steps to widen the distance between me and Lurlene.

"I think we've been invaded," he said. "By galactic geeks."

I slapped his arm, suppressing a giggle.

He continued to stare for an extra long moment. Then he said, "Well, see you around, Keller." He turned and shot one more look at Lurlene before sprinting off down the hall.

"Wow," Lurlene breathed in my ear. "Is he your boyfriend?"

I shook my head. "Not a chance. He's the hottest guy in school."

"I think he likes you."

"Oh, yeah. He's big on nerds."

She laughed, that obnoxious laugh that carried down the hall.

Brad glanced back. My cheeks burned neon red, I'm sure. Whirling around, I scurried off in the opposite direction. "Come on, Lurlene. We'd better find your first class."

"I'm right behind you," she said.

Good. Just stay there, I thought.

4

I told Lurlene I'd leave a little early between classes to help her locate her rooms. It was no big deal, but she seemed so grateful, I thought she was going to hug me.

Get real.

I hadn't thought about what to do with her at lunch, probably because the thought of it made me sick. Out of habit, when the lunch bell rang, I raced from the gym to the cafeteria. Late again. Kimberly would be irritated if our table was already occupied. It was the most remote one in the corner, where we could dodge most of the airborne peas from food fights while we worked. As I clutched my dictionary to my chest and squealed around the corner, I almost had a rear-end collision with Lurlene.

My eyes darted wildly for a place to hide. No closets, no alleys, no luck. I held my hand over my eyebrows and lowered my head, hoping if I couldn't see her, she couldn't see me. Stupid.

"Ann!" she called, loud enough for everyone on the planet to hear. "Here I am."

I cringed.

"I hope you weren't waiting for me very long," she said.

"No. I wasn't waiting." The truth, at least.

"You're going to have to show me how to do this. It's a buffet, right? Like Furr's cafeteria? We used to go to Furr's once a month with my grandparents — when we were still a family."

I wished she'd stop saying that. The look on her face made me swallow hard.

"Okay, Lurlene," I interrupted her mental trek to family day at Furr's. "Just follow me into the cafeteria and do what I do. Don't talk — just stay behind me, okay?"

She clamped her jaw and looked at me.

"I mean, unless you see food move. Then scream and run."

Her face softened, and she smiled.

There was this foot dangling from my mouth, but I had more unsavory things to think about. This was going to be tricky. I hoped no one I knew would be eating that day.

With an audible sigh of resignation, I pushed open the swinging doors of the Shiffley Middle School cafeteria. Hundreds of people were weaving between tables, screaming at friends, throwing food and silverware. Nothing unusual until . . .

I felt the stares starting. Then the din took a plunge. People began to whisper together and snicker. "Hey, geek," someone said out loud. The hairs on my neck stood at attention.

Jennifer Caldwell grabbed my arm. Besides being head cheerleader, she's a royal snob. I can't stand her, except I wouldn't mind having her hair, her body, her clothes.

"Ann, don't look now, but Pee Wee Herman's twin sister just lined up behind you." She leaned against me, howling.

I forced a grim chuckle.

"Ow," I heard Lurlene say. "Let go."

Turning, I saw that Brad McKenzie had approached from the rear and was tugging one of Lurlene's pigtails. When her eyes met mine, they pleaded for help. I just couldn't. I was frozen in place. Thankfully, Brad flashed a smile at me and took off.

The line moved forward, and I lurched with it. I picked up a tray and out of the corner of my eye watched Lurlene follow suit. Although the whispering continued from the people in line, at least we were hidden behind the buffet counter from the hecklers in the lunchroom. It was safe enough to speak.

In a low voice I explained to Lurlene how things worked. There were two buffets, one for hot meals and one for salads. Also, she could get prepackaged sandwiches, cookies, and chips. The desserts were at another counter by the drinks. On Fridays Taco Bell and McDonald's brought in real food. I was trying not to move my lips.

As we inched forward, I said, "The special today is Salisbury steak. Basically that's grilled roadkill with suicide sauce. I don't recommend it. The salads are okay, but the sandwiches are risky, especially the green liverwurst."

She started to laugh.

I held up a hand. "I usually have pizza or a cheeseburger," I added quickly. "What sounds good to you?"

Her eyes grew wide and her mouth wide-open as she surveyed the cafeteria layout. "This is so amazing," she said. "I . . . I guess I'll have a cheeseburger."

"I just lost my appetite." Jennifer Caldwell clicked by us in her new Georgios. She tossed a brown apple core onto Lurlene's tray.

Granted, Lurlene was a geek, but that was offensive. Narrowing my eyes at Jennifer's receding back, I said, "Just ignore her. Jennifer Caldwell's a jerk."

Instead of smiling gratefully at me, Lurlene said, "So

she's a jerk, you're a nerd, and I'm a geek. Is anyone around here just a normal person?"

I met her eyes. "No," I said. "We're all pretty much nerds and geeks and jerks."

She burst into laughter. I squinched and tried to melt into the ice cream freezer.

We ordered our burgers, grabbed a milk and a piece of pie, then stood in line to pay. My lunch rang in at $2.05. I picked up my tray and searched for Kimberly. Behind me, the cashier repeated, "Two-oh-five."

Then, "*Two-oh-five*. Come on. You're holding up the line."

I glanced over my shoulder. Lurlene just stood there, red-faced. Instantly I surmised the problem.

"Oops, sorry," I told the cashier. "I forgot it was my turn to pay. We sort of alternate." I set down my tray and scrounged in my bag for another two dollars and change.

"Thank you, Ann," she whispered, looking embarrassed. "I thought the food was free," she said. "I thought, since it's public school —"

"Forget it. There's Kimberly." I pointed with my chin. "Come on, follow me." I took a deep breath. Just keep your distance, Lurlene, okay? I prayed to myself.

It was like walking through a snake pit, all the hissing and recoiling. An eternity later, we arrived at the corner table, where Kimberly was buried in her dictionary. I sat down and motioned Lurlene to sit across from me. Kimberly raised her head. "Sorry, this table's taken," she said to Lurlene.

"She's with me," I answered.

Kimberly's eyes doubled in size behind her thick lenses.

"Kimberly, this is Lurlene. Lurlene, my best friend, Kimberly."

"Hi," Lurlene said. "It must be great to have Ann as a friend. She's so funny."

"A real scream," Kimberly said flatly. I sneered. She sipped her milk and stared at Lurlene. Finally Kimberly dropped the empty carton on her tray, thrust her dictionary at me, and pointed with a stiff finger. "Start on *onomatopoeia*."

"I can't believe these cheeseburgers. They're bigger than Dad's buffalo burgers." Lurlene bit ferociously into her burger.

"Do you mind?" Kimberly said. "We're trying to concentrate."

Lurlene looked across the table at me with wounded eyes.

"We're practicing," I explained, "for the spelling bee."

"Oh," Lurlene said.

"Just ignore us," I told her. Turning to Kimberly, I repeated, "On-uh-mot-uh-PEE-uh. Definition: 'The naming of a thing or action by a vocal imitation of the sound associated with it.' What?" I looked up. "I don't get it."

Lurlene said, "Like *buzz* or *hiss*. Like *meeeooow*." It came out real loud. People searched around their seats for the cat.

I hid my head, and my smile. It was kind of funny. Kimberly assumed her fiercest warrior expression. "*Onomatopoeia*. O-n-o-m-a-t-o-p-o-e-i-a," she spelled.

"Correctamundo." I slid the dictionary back to her.

Kimberly found the place and read, "*Ontogeny*. On-TOJ-en-ee. The development or course of development especially of an individual organism." Kimberly pushed her glasses up her nose. "Do you need a sentence?"

"I'd prefer an individual organism to develop right here. Preferably male. Preferably Brad McKenzie."

Lurlene choked on her cheeseburger. She came up for air, howling. Kimberly glared. Sucking in a smile, I spelled, "O-n-t-o-g-e-n-y. *Ontogeny*."

The dictionary passed back to me. "Okay. *Onyx*," I said.

"Too easy. Give me a harder one."

I searched the page, then flipped to the next.

"*Ophidian*. Oh-FID-ee-un. 'Of, relating to, or resembling snakes.' " I turned to Lurlene.

She caught my eye and said, "Hissss."

We both giggled.

Kimberly stared, deadpan. She spelled, "O-p-h-i-d-e-a-n. *Ophidean*."

"Errrrrrt. It's d-i-a-n."

Kimberly ripped off a shred of lettuce and gnashed it

between her teeth. Then she yanked the dictionary from me. "There's nothing else in the *OP*'s. Let's start on *OR*'s. Here. *Ordnance*. Military supplies."

I thought it meant something else, like a law. "*Ordnance*," I repeated. "O-r-d-i-n-a-n-c-e."

"Errrrrt," Lurlene buzzed.

Kimberly and I shifted our eyes to her.

"O-r-d-*n*-a-n-c-e," she spelled. "No *i*."

I turned back to Kimberly, questioning, and she confirmed. "She's right. There's no *i* in this one."

"How did you know, Lurlene?" I asked before chomping into my cheeseburger.

She shrugged and chomped into her cheeseburger, too.

Kimberly and I continued with *ordure, organoleptic, origanum,* and *ormolu.* Quiet as a mole, Lurlene finished her lunch. Everything was fine until . . .

"*Osteoporosis*. O-s-t-e-o —"

"My grandmother has that," Lurlene interrupted Kimberly. "She's starting to get a hunchback, too. Dad suggested we ship her off to Notre Dame. Mom didn't think that was funny."

I did. I burst out laughing.

Lurlene beamed. Then she broke into laughter and heaved so hard heads turned.

Kimberly stood up. "Let's get some milk, Ann," she said, and I rose with her. As we stood in line, I saw Lurlene pick up her milk, examine it, then open both ends.

"She is horrible, Ann," Kimberly whispered. "How long are you stuck with her?"

"Just until she can find her way around. Maybe another day. I'm supposed to help her fit in."

"Good luck." Kimberly shuddered beside me.

We both stared at the table, where Lurlene twisted a pigtail around her hand while leafing through the dictionary. "She's not as bad as she looks," I said.

Kimberly arched an eyebrow at me. "How do you spell *geek?*"

She was right. *Geek,* from the Greek for "eek."

After paying for our milks, we meandered ever so slowly back to the table. I resolved to rid myself of Lurlene Brueggemeyer by lunchtime tomorrow. The longer we hung out together, the harder it would be to dump her. People might start to associate us. Even though she laughed at my jokes, which was kind of flattering, I was afraid Lurlene might start to think we could be friends.

5

A message had been scribbled on the blackboard when I arrived at study hall. ALL-SCHOOL ASSEMBLY. TODAY AT 1:30. REQUIRED ATTENDANCE.

All right! That should take a nice chunk out of algebra class. I flipped back to the *OS's* in my dictionary and scanned the page. *Ostracize.* "To exclude from a group by common consent." I wondered if Lurlene realized that was happening to her. *Ostrich.* Was I sticking my head in the sand by not defending her? *Otiose.* "Producing no useful effect." Sentence: As a sponsor, Ann Keller is otiose.

I slammed the dictionary closed. Behind Mr. Howell's scowl, the bell for the assembly sounded. Along with everyone else, I scrambled to my locker to relieve myself of books, especially one algebra text and one *Webster's* dictionary. Then I followed the mob to the gymnasium.

The bleachers were pulled out, and folding chairs were set up on the floor. I looked around for Kimberly. "Ann, over here." That familiar voice.

When I turned, Lurlene was waving to me from the front row of chairs. I balked.

"There's that geek," someone said behind me. "Who's she waving to?"

Instinctively I ducked behind a group of people on their way in. "Ann, hi. Want to sit with us?" Sara Chen, my next-door neighbor, pulled up beside me with a couple of her friends.

"Sure. Unless Kimberly —"

"Hey, look. There's that creepy new girl. Ooh, she is so weird," Sara said.

As we passed by, Lurlene called, "Ann. Ann!" but I pretended not to hear. I climbed the bleachers with Sara. Below, just coming through the door, was Kimberly.

"Kimberly, up here," I yelled. She waved and bounded up the bleachers. My eyes caught Lurlene's, and for a long moment we locked gazes. Then Lurlene turned around and plopped down in a chair.

The gym kept filling up while we chattered and passed notes around. My eyes kept straying to the front row, where Lurlene was sitting all alone. The whole row was empty. "Come on," I said under my breath. "Somebody sit with her." Then it happened. The worst possible thing.

"Look at that," Sara said. "Can you believe it?"

I couldn't. It was bad for Lurlene. In full view of the whole school, Mrs. Welter sat down right next to her. She and Lurlene talked for a minute, then like a videocam Mrs. Welter pivoted her head and zoomed in on me. Oh, man. I wanted to slither down the back of the bleachers and out of that scene.

The assembly was about not doing drugs, again, for the bejillionth time this year. An ex-con got up and told his story, which was supposed to scare the stoners into going straight. Unfortunately most of them were in the rest rooms smoking.

Lurlene looked sufficiently shocked. She was about the only one. Afterward, Mrs. Welter got up onstage and announced that Kimberly and I were representing the school at the Denver County spelling bee. She made us stand up, which was utterly humiliating.

When the assembly was over, Kimberly and I slunk out into the hall. "Are we practicing tonight?" she asked, both of us trying to fade into the brickwork. "We need to get an early start, because I have my church youth group at eight. We're not making very good progress, you know. We didn't get anywhere at lunch today. You know why."

I rolled my eyes, but she didn't notice. "I'll come over right after dinner."

"Good." She glanced at her watch. "Look, I'm going to spend a half hour or so in the library. We could get through a good part of the *P*'s. Want to come?"

I peered around the door into the almost empty gym. "No, you go ahead. I have some other stuff to do."

She shrugged. "See you tonight, then." Her long legs carried her swiftly down the hall and out of view.

I took a deep breath and headed back into the gym. "Hi, Ann. Bye, Ann." Brad McKenzie brushed past me at the door. We actually touched arms. Tingle city. "Where you going? The nerd herd went that-a-way." He thumbed over his shoulder.

"Shut up," I muttered.

He grinned. "You coming to the game tonight?"

I weaseled in place. "Actually, I, uh . . ."

"Yeah, I know. Spelling."

I smiled weakly.

"Later, then. Nerrrrd."

Cringing, I thought, I wish he wouldn't call me that. When he crinkled his blue eyes at me, though, I instantly forgave him. I stalled in the hall until he disappeared, then snuck through the doors.

She was standing in front of the stage, talking to Mrs. Welter. "Lurlene," I called. "Hey, where were you? I looked everywhere before the assembly." I rushed across the gym. "Oh, hi, Mrs. Welter."

"Ann," Mrs. Welter said. "I was just asking Lurlene how things are going."

Lurlene and I looked at each other. "Everything's fine." Lurlene blinked back to the principal. "Ann's the perfect sponsor. She's teaching me a lot of things about public school. If you'll excuse me, I have to go. I wouldn't want to miss a minute of 'Math for the Mental Giant.' " Through her thin smile there was not a glint of metal. She headed for the exit.

"She's such a nice girl, isn't she?" Mrs. Welter said.

Unlike some people, you mean? I didn't say it. I felt it.

"So, tell me Ann. Are you ready for the next round?"

"Of what?"

"Spelling."

"Oh. Kimberly'll win," I replied automatically. The sea of students parted as Lurlene plowed into the crowded corridor.

"Maybe *you'll* win this year. I expect to see both of you at the Colorado state spelling bee."

My attention veered back to Mrs. Welter. "What?"

"I said, maybe you'll win."

I gave a short laugh. "Don't bet money on it."

"Think positively, Ann." She escorted me toward the door. "Why, I'm already planning an assembly to celebrate. A sort of pep rally." Pausing, she thrust her fist into the air. "Three cheers for Ann Keller. National Spelling Bee champion. *Whoop, whoop, whoop.*" She made little circles with her fist.

Okay, Mrs. Welter, I thought. The air is pretty thin up there.

She thrust my fist skyward. "Come on."

"*Whoop,*" I mimicked, with about as much enthusiasm as a whooping crane with whooping cough.

6

D day. Ditch Lurlene day. Yesterday, on my way out after school, I'd shoved a note in Lurlene's locker telling her I'd meet her there in the morning, since it was closer to both our classrooms. She didn't know it yet, but it was the last time we were going to meet. Anywhere.

When I got to her locker the next morning, Lurlene wasn't waiting as expected. She was nowhere to be seen or heard. Reluctantly I took up my casual stance — nonchalantly lounging against the wall, examining my nails.

The hall began to swarm, and still no sign of Lurlene. I was just about to blow her off when the east door swung open and *it* appeared.

The apparition was cloaked in a pink-and-green plaid coat, but that wasn't the scary part. The shivers started with the ski mask pulled down all the way. The kind with eye and mouth slits?

My stomach plunged. For the first time ever, I was thankful to be short as I wove through the crowd and out of there.

All during history, I couldn't stop thinking about Lurlene. Don't ask me why. Every time I tried to bury her in my brain, she burrowed back up. Like a kaleidoscope, she appeared in full living color.

What kind of sponsor was I? The worst kind, I decided. Otiose. But so what? I never asked for the job.

As Dr. Ramirez traced the outline of the Louisiana Purchase on the wall-size map up front, I thought history. Think history. Lurlene Brueggemeyer is history.

"Ms. Keller, do you know the answer?"

"History."

"Excuse me?" he said.

"Uh, what was the question?" My face felt as red as Baton Rouge.

Dr. Ramirez glared at me over his wire-rims. Thankfully I was saved by the bell.

After class I went by Lurlene's first period class, where I knew she'd be waiting. She was probably sorry she'd missed me this morning, probably frantic to apologize.

The classroom was empty. No Lurlene.

I altered my usual route and wandered by her next class. No Lurlene.

In fact, I didn't see her all morning. I decided fate had intervened. Obviously Lurlene didn't need a sponsor anymore. Problem solved. Case closed.

On my way to lunch, I was still thinking about her. Why? It was giving me indigestion. I figured I had a pretty good excuse not to eat with her now. After all, she'd been avoiding me all morning — the revelation jolted me. Was that true? Was Lurlene avoiding *me*?

I turned the corner, expecting her to pounce at the cafeteria doors. Muscles tensed. No Lurlene.

"What are you doing, Ann?" a voice sounded behind me. "Waiting for your geeky friend?" Jennifer Caldwell and her groupies swarmed past.

"Yeah, right." So what *was* I doing?

"She's not coming," Jennifer said. "I think she went home sick."

One of the groupies added, "I thought she went home ugly." They collapsed in hysterics as they barreled through the cafeteria doors en masse.

I wasn't glad Lurlene was sick, exactly, but a long exhale of relief escaped my lips.

Eating lunch alone with Kimberly would be like old times. Even though it'd only been a day and a half, pre-Lurlene seemed a prehistoric era. I promised myself I wasn't going to think about her. "What is this glop to-day?" I said, sliding in across from Kimberly and gazing down into my tray. Little pieces of hamburger (I hoped

44

that's what it was) oozed over the ridge of a mashed potato crater. "Lava melt?" I ventured.

Kimberly didn't even flinch. She stared at the dictionary page, mouthing a word. Even as she took a bite of tuna sandwich, she closed her eyes and spelled to herself.

"Kimberly?" I waved a spoon in front of her face. "You have company."

"Start here." She slid the book across to me. "At *periodontal*."

"Could we just eat first?" I looked beseechingly at her. "My volcano's erupting here, and so is my stomach."

She pulled the book back. "You go ahead. You don't mind if I work, do you? I mean, I've got this schedule —"

"Yeah, I know. The dreaded schedule. Go ahead."

She read another word to herself, chomped, and closed her eyes.

As I watched, the lava gravy congealed. Gag. I bit into my brownie and remembered something. "My mom called last night. She said there's a realtors' convention in the Springs this weekend and she can't have me and Chase come stay. *Again*. This is like the third week in a row."

Kimberly pushed her glasses up her nose and flipped a page.

"Did you hear me?"

"Mmm," she responded. "Pair-uh-puh-TET-ik. *Peripatetic*."

"My life is peri-*pathetic*," I snarled. "But never mind. Maybe in the next one I'll come back as the invisible woman. Not that anyone'd notice."

Kimberly blinked up.

I guessed I had her attention. As I dug a walnut out of my brownie, I said, "The only reason she's going is so she'll have a legitimate excuse not to come to Chase's wrestling meet. Then, last night Dad stood in front of the fireplace and burned all his old love letters to Mom. One at a time. It made me want to cry."

"Could you get me another milk?" Kimberly said.

"What?"

"I don't want to lose my place." She handed me a dollar.

Steaming, I scraped my chair across the linoleum and stormed to the drink line. "She didn't hear a word I said," I muttered under my breath. As I paid for the milk, I studied her, all hunched over the dictionary. Read, chomp, spell. Read, chomp, spell. Geez, she was possessed.

I bought a chocolate milk and went back. With a heavy sigh, I plopped into my seat and handed the carton to Kimberly. No change for the dollar. When she asked for it, I was planning to say, "Sorry, slave wages have gone up." But she didn't even give me the pleasure of asking. After five minutes, I gave it back to her anyway.

Five minutes later, I reached across and slammed the dictionary closed.

"Hey!"

"Kimberly, talk to me. What's going on? This spelling bee has taken over your life."

"No, it hasn't." She clucked. Her eyes strayed down to the milk carton, and she opened it. "I just want to be champion," she mumbled. "Like Janet Evans in swimming or Shannon Miller in gymnastics. Mom's right. If I work extra hard, there's a good chance I could be the National Spelling Bee champion." She pushed up her glasses.

I watched her eyes gaze past me to the wall before they glazed over completely, and I wondered, What did she think? That if she won she was going to get her face on a box of Wheaties?

I had to snap her out of it. "So, do you want to go to Pizza Hut before the wrestling meet on Saturday? Think your mom'd let you stay over if you promised her you'd be home early for church? Just this once?"

Kimberly focused in on me. "Saturday?"

It took all my resolve not to lunge across the table and strangle her. "Saturday. Wrestling? Chase? High school? Pizza? Sleep over? Any of that ring a bell?"

"This Saturday?" she said. "I can't. It's my mom and dad's anniversary, and we're all going out to Gasho for dinner. Afterward, the Colorado Symphony is having a free concert. It's family night."

"Family night," I repeated.

"And Sunday I need to practice. All day." She met my narrowed eyes. "I mean, we both do. You could come over, if you want." Her voice trailed off.

Well, that was a weak invitation if I ever heard one. In the most level voice I could manage, I said, "I'll think about it."

I didn't see Lurlene on Thursday or Friday. I wondered if she really was sick, or if, like me, she was faking it to avoid something unpleasant. Say school, or her sponsor.

Here I was thinking about Lurlene again. Probably because Kimberly had all but abandoned me. What was I to her anyway? A coach? A groupie? Surely not a friend. I couldn't even talk to her, she was such a robot. Work, work, work. She'd been stung by the spelling bee, and the venom was fatal.

Saturday night I went with Dad to Chase's wrestling meet. Dad spotted one of his clients, so he dragged me halfway up the bleachers to sit with them. They had a son Chase's age who wrestled heavyweight. We're talking sumo.

Just as the first match got under way, a vision caught my eyes. A familiar color combination, pink and green, at the open gymnasium doors. It was Lurlene, surrounded by little kids, and an older lady I presumed was her mother. "Dad, I'll be back." He stood with me and pulled out a five dollar bill from his wallet. "Get me a couple of hot dogs," he said. "With everything on 'em."

"Do I look like your slave?"

He studied me. "Well . . ."

I slugged him. Obviously I was this year's slave of the universe.

Lurlene was hunched over the drinking fountain when I got there. "Hey, Lurlene," I said behind her. "How're you feeling?"

Her head shot up. Water dribbled down her chin, and she swiped it away. "Hi, Ann." Her face lit up, or maybe it was wishful thinking on my part. No, she seemed genuinely happy to see me before a voice said, "Lurlene?" Her demeanor suddenly changed. She lowered her eyes to the mats. "This is my mom. My brothers . . ." She rattled off a roster of names so fast it sounded as if she were speaking Swahili.

"Hi." I hailed a group greeting.

"I'm going to find us a place to sit so we can watch Bud," her mother said. "You sit with your friend if you want." She squeezed Lurlene's shoulder and smiled at me. The Brueggemeyer bunch trooped off toward the bleachers. Lurlene's mom was tall, big-boned like Lurlene, sort of earthy in her Birkenstocks with argyle kneesocks.

"I have to get my dad a couple of hot dogs," I told

Lurlene. She nodded and followed me back out to the hall. We lined up at the makeshift concession stand, a long table set up in front of the trophy case. "I missed you these last couple of days."

Her eyes met mine. "You did?"

I gulped and hoped she couldn't detect my nose growing. "You must've been really sick."

She gave me a funny look. "Who told you I was sick?"

"Uh . . . I don't remember." Another inch of schnoz.

"On Wednesday I had achievement tests all day," she said. "Remember, I told you?"

Did she? It must've been during one of those times I'd blocked her out, which was most of the time.

"Then Thursday and Friday I had to stay home and baby-sit while Mom went out job hunting." Lurlene sighed.

I knew that sigh.

"Whaddya want?"

"Two hot dogs with the works," I said to the zitty kid behind the table. "How long have your parents been divorced?" I asked Lurlene while the kid slathered the buns.

"About three months. Since right before Christmas. Dad moved to Florida, so I'll probably never see him again." She paused and smiled grimly. "How about you?"

I counted. "Eight months now. My mom moved to Colorado Springs, which might as well be Florida. She and my dad hate each other's guts. They don't talk."

Lurlene shook her head. "I'll never understand how two people can be all happy and normal one day, then the next day everything's changed between them."

"I know exactly what you mean!" We talked about how things had changed. How our lives were different. "I hate having two homes," I said. "I hate lugging my stereo back and forth."

"I hate the home I have," Lurlene said.

As we wandered back to the bleachers, I asked, "Which wrestler's your brother?"

"The skinny one with the hairy chest." Lurlene pointed. He did have a hairy chest. Otherwise, he was kind of cute.

"Chase, that's my brother," I motioned with a hot dog. "The one with the hairy head. Chase! Hey, Chase!" I lived to embarrass him.

He obliged with a blush.

"Let me dump these off and we can sit together." I started up the bleachers.

Lurlene yanked me back by the sweater. "I better help Mom out," she said. My eyes followed hers to the end of the bleachers, where her little brothers were playing Mighty Morphins up and down the risers. Lurlene's mom looked tired. "I'll see you Monday," Lurlene said. "I *hope*, if Mom gets that job she wants at Denver General."

"She's a nurse?"

"Doctor," Lurlene replied. "But she gave up her practice

when she had us kids. Now she's been out of medicine for a long time, and she's having trouble finding a job. Dad sends money but —" Lurlene sighed again. Cupping her hands over her mouth, she hollered across the mats, "Get back here, Billy Ray! Darryl, go get him." I watched her clomp off. Boy, I thought, compared to her life, mine's cake.

7

Lurlene never showed at her locker Monday morning. I figured she was still stuck with baby-sitting duty, poor kid. That's why it surprised me so much when she appeared at our lunch table. I dropped my burrito when I saw her. "Hey, Lurlene, hi." I slid my tray over so she could set hers down.

Kimberly gave me a look.

I gave her one back.

"Your mom get the job?" I asked Lurlene.

"She doesn't know yet, but she found some temporary day care for my brothers. Thank gawwwd." Lurlene rolled her eyes.

I giggled.

Kimberly said, "Can we please get back to spelling?" She drummed her fingernails on the table.

I said to Lurlene, "Hope you're ready for another exciting lunchroom spell-down."

She garbled through a mouthful of chips, "Mmmm, go ahead. I won't bother you. By the way," she reached into the breast pocket of her flannel shirt, "here's the money I owe you for lunch last week. With interest."

"Lurlene, you didn't have to do that."

She handed me three dollars. "I bought you a new spelling notebook, too, since I wrote in yours. It's in my locker. Maybe after lunch we can stop and get it —"

"Ann, start here," Kimberly cut her off. She pointed near the end of a page.

I looked at the word and muttered, "Oh, that's appropriate."

Lurlene peered over the top of the dictionary. She sucked in a smile.

"*Regurgitate*," I read out loud. "To toss up cookies. To vomit. Upchuck. Like this." I faked a good one.

Lurlene whooped with laughter.

Kimberly made a sick face. She rattled off, "R-e-g-u-r-j-i-t-a-t-e. *Regurjitate*."

"Errrrt," Lurlene buzzed.

Kimberly narrowed her eyes at her.

"She's right," I said.

"Then *you* spell it," she snapped at Lurlene.

Lurlene shrugged. "*Regurgitate*. R-e-g-u-r-g-i-t-a-t-e. *Regurgitate*."

"That's what I said."

"No, you didn't," I informed Kimberly. "You said g-u-r-*j*."

Kimberly looked at Lurlene, who lowered her eyes and crunched another potato chip.

Kimberly grabbed the dictionary from me. "You're making me lose my concentration. Spell *rehabilitate, Ann.*"

"Ree-uh-BIL-uh-tate?" I couldn't picture it.

Kimberly used my stall to think up a sentence. "You can't expect to rehabilitate the hopeless." She waited.

I exhaled a breath. "R-e-a —"

Lurlene coughed over my *a*. "I had a friend who used to live in a rehab house," she said. "It was built by Habitat for Humanity."

"Ohhhh." I nodded. "Ree-HUH-bil-uh-tate. Why didn't you say so, Kimberly?"

She muttered, "It has two pronunciations."

And you picked the most obscure. Thanks a lot. I didn't say it. I spelled the word right.

"It was the neatest house," Lurlene said. "Her bed pulled right out of the wall."

Kimberly rose. "I'm going for dessert," she said, leaving abruptly.

Lurlene bit her knuckle. "She's mad. I'm sorry. I didn't mean to make her mad." She glanced worriedly across the cafeteria.

"She'll get over it. Lurlene, tell me how you knew those words."

"I don't know." She shrugged. "We used to have dictionary drills for our spelling lesson sometimes. And we played a lot of Scrabble. Dad said once that he thought I had a photographic memory." Lurlene frowned across the room again. "Ann, I don't want Kimberly to be mad at you because of me."

"She's not. She's just upset because she misspelled a word. This contest is really important to her. Too important." My eyes followed Lurlene's to where Kimberly was counting out change for milk. "Lurlene"— I turned back to her —"you should be in the spelling bee. You're really good."

She blushed. "No, I'm not."

"Yes, you are. If you have a photographic memory, that makes you a natural."

She thought about it for a minute. "What do you get if you win?"

"You get to go to Washington, D.C. If you win the state competition, that is. Then, if you win the National Spelling Bee, you get to meet the president and be on all the talk shows, MTV. Fame and fortune."

Her eyes lit up. "How do I enter?"

"Well . . ." At this point I wasn't sure she could. The school contests were over, and the area spelling bees had already qualified the finalists for county. But the organizers would just have to make an exception for Lurlene. She was a speller. "Come with us to the county spelling bee. It's in two weeks. All you have to do is sign up at the door," I fibbed. I'd fix it somehow.

"Would I have to compete against you?" she asked.

"Yeah. And Kimberly. Of course, neither one of us would have a chance against her. But it'd be fun if all three of us could go." What was I saying? Fun? Kimberly would kill me. As in m-u-r-d-e-r.

Lurlene slurped on her milk. "Maybe I will enter. If it's just for fun."

Kimberly came back. She sat down stiffly and took the dictionary from my hands. "So, Lurlene. Try this one. Rih-joo-vuh-NESS-ens."

"Come on, Kimberly," I said. "Forget it."

"No, Ann. I want her to spell it."

Lurlene scrunched her eyebrows together. "That's a hard one. Let's see." I could tell she was flipping through her mental dictionary. "Rih-joo-vuh-NESS-ens. R-e-j-u-v-e-n-e-s-c-e-n-c-e?"

Kimberly's eyes locked on mine. Shock. Now was not the time to tell her we were taking Lurlene to the spelling bee.

Kimberly actually called and asked me to come over that evening. To spell, of course, but that was okay. At least we were still friends.

Sprawled across her bed with the dictionary spread open on my chest, I said, "What would you say if I sort of encouraged Lurlene to enter the spelling bee?"

"I'd say with friends like you, who needs enemies?"

"That's not fair, Kimberly." I shot upright. "Anyone can enter. It's a free country, you know."

"It's too late. The qualifying rounds are over."

"I bet they'd make an exception for her. Since she was in home school and couldn't compete."

Kimberly just looked at me.

"She worries you, doesn't she?"

"That's ridiculous." Kimberly swiveled around on her desk chair. "I just don't want to hang out with her. And you shouldn't either. People are starting to talk, Ann."

That locked my jaw in gape-open position. "Who's talking?"

"Everyone. Brad McKenzie. What's the next word?"

I whapped the dictionary closed in my lap. "What about Brad McKenzie?"

"You lost our place!" Kimberly cried. "Give me the dictionary if you don't want to practice."

"Not until you tell me what you heard."

Kimberly sighed wearily. "Jennifer Caldwell said she heard Brad McKenzie was going to ask you out, but every time he saw you, you were with that geek. I assume he meant Lurlene."

I bolted to my feet. "Are you kidding? He wants to

ask me out? I'm not really hanging out with her. I mean, maybe it looks that way, but I'm just showing her around. I *have* to. I'm her sponsor. You told Jennifer that, didn't you?"

Kimberly didn't reply. "The dictionary, please?" she said.

"Kimberly, you did tell Jennifer that I'm Lurlene's sponsor." I held the book away from her grubby little hands.

"I think Lurlene knows her way around now. Look, Ann, my advice is just stay away from her. Tell her to get lost."

"I can't! I promised Mrs. Welter. And besides, she — I . . ." I stopped short, my voice trailing off.

Kimberly frowned and shook her head. "It's your reputation. I'd appreciate it, though, if you'd keep her away from me."

"No problem." I tossed the dictionary behind me onto the bed.

"Where are you going?" she said.

"Home." I shoved my clenched fists into the armholes of my ski parka.

"Well, thanks a lot. I thought you were going to start me through the *S*'s tonight."

Storming to the bedroom door, I turned and said, "You don't need me, Kimberly. Start yourself through the *S*'s." And I slammed the door behind me.

*   *   *

59

The next morning as I approached Lurlene's locker, I spied a banner draped across the corridor. GO, BULLETS. SLAM-DUNK LAKE MIDDLE SCHOOL. Suddenly my feet felt like they were slogging through quicksand. Slower, slower. Why *was* I still meeting Lurlene? I wondered. Maybe Kimberly was right; Lurlene could find her way around. Even if she did decide to spell with us at lunch, we didn't need to be together all the time. There was my reputation to consider. There was Brad McKenzie to consider.

I made my decision. Run. Too late, the east door flew open and cowboy boots clomped in. The urge to bolt was strong, but for some reason, my feet refused to respond to my brain.

"Hi, Ann!" Lurlene hollered, waving from the door.

I tossed back a weak wave.

"Look. I got a new schedule yesterday." She plowed up the hall and handed me a crumpled piece of paper. As she spun the combination on her lock, I smoothed the schedule across my notebook.

My eyes widened. "Is this for real?" I asked. "You're in all the advanced classes."

Lurlene flashed her reflecto smile. "I know. Mrs. Welter said my test scores were outstanding." She elbowed me. "I guess that makes me a nerd like you."

"I guess," I mumbled as I studied her schedule more

closely. My throat constricted. "You have four classes with me."

"Really? Maybe we can sit together."

I opened my mouth, but no words came out. I wondered if I could transfer to Colorado Springs halfway through the semester.

"Hi, Ann." That voice. I plastered a smile on my face and spun around.

"Oh, hi, Brad."

"Can I walk you to class?"

Lurlene's locker clanged shut. I felt her move up next to me. Brad's eyes shifted over.

"Hi," she said to him.

He coughed.

She snapped her fingers. "Ann, I just remembered. I left my notebook in the gym. I'll see you in history class." She plodded off down the hall, her pigtails flaring like fishtails. From about a hundred feet away, she pivoted and yelled, "Save me a seat, okay?"

A thousand eyes turned to stare. A thousand deaths I died.

"Are you two friends?" Brad asked. His wide blue eyes made me blush.

I forced a laugh. "Very funny. I'm just her sponsor. I'm supposed to show her around."

He shuddered. "Poor thing."

I gazed past him to Lurlene's disappearing back. "Yeah, really."

"Not her. You." He grabbed my books and started down the hall. I smiled, and scrambled to catch up. Then I thought of something. Lurlene didn't have gym. Why would her notebook be in the gym? And how was she ever going to find our history class clear out in the annex?

8

Somehow Lurlene made it to the annex without my help, and even though I felt guilty about stranding her, my reason seemed justified. Lurlene must've thought so with her disappearing act. Brad. Sigh. I could still feel the fireworks.

It turned out Lurlene and I had history and English together in the morning, then algebra and keyboarding in the afternoon. Every class but gym.

I wasn't sure how I was going to handle all this togetherness and still pretend Lurlene was a wart on my world. Mostly because I didn't really feel that way. Luckily Brad wasn't in any of my classes.

When I rushed into the cafeteria after gym, Lurlene was already there, saving the table. No Kimberly, though.

Then it struck me; Kimberly hadn't been in English that morning either. Did she tell me she was going to be gone? No. She must be sick, I thought. Probably from stress. Not that I wished it were true, but her absence was kind of a blessing. I wouldn't have to worry about playing mediator.

First thing Lurlene asked was, "Where's Kimberly?"

"Who knows?"

She studied my face. "Are you mad at her?

I shifted in my chair. "A little bit. I guess we had kind of a fight." I wondered if Kimberly was even aware of it.

"What about?" Lurlene said.

About you, I almost blurted. "Nothing. Just stupid stuff." I lifted my corn dog and bit off the end.

"I hope you make up. Friends shouldn't fight, especially best friends. I mean, who else are you going to talk to? It's so hard to find a really good friend."

I swallowed hard, pushing back the rising lump in my throat. When I didn't respond, Lurlene piped up, "Do you want to practice spelling?"

I groaned.

She smiled. "We don't have to."

"No, we'd better." I unzipped my backpack and lugged out the old *Webster's*. "Guess you decided to enter."

She nodded. "Washington D.C.'s not too far from Florida. Maybe my dad could meet me there." Her eyes glinted as bright as her braces. I hated to break the news to her — the likelihood that she was going to beat Kimberly and get to Washington, D.C., was like less than zero. "Let me give you the first word," she said. She opened the dictionary to my dog-eared page.

"*Sabbatical*," she read. " 'A break or change from a normal routine.' A sentence. Hmm . . ." She thought for a minute. "I wish I could take a permanent sabbatical from algebra."

I clucked. "No kidding. *Sabbatical*. S-a-b-b-a-t-i-c-a-l. *Sabbatical*."

"Good!"

Wow. Was that praise? My flagging spirits billowed a bit. "My turn." I spun the dictionary around. "SAY-bin. *Sabin*. 'A unit of acoustic absorption equivalent to the absorption by one square foot of a perfect absorber.' Huh? Did you absorb any of that?"

She laughed. "Are you sabin that cookie for later?" She pointed to my tray.

I chuckled and passed her the cookie.

"Thanks," she said. "*Sabin*. S-a-b-i-n."

"That's right. Lurlene, you're amazing. Okay, give me a word. A hard one."

She slid the dictionary around. "Try . . . sak-uh-RIM-uh-ter."

"Saca who?"

"*Saccharimeter*. Or if I say it like it's spelled, sak-CHAR-i-meet-er."

65

I narrowed eyes at her. "I think that's cheating."

Grinning, she bit into the cookie.

"But thanks." I took a deep breath. "S-a-c-c-h-a-r-i-m-e-t-e-r."

"Right!"

"Well, well. Isn't this cozy?" Jennifer Caldwell loomed over us with a trayful of trash. Her groupie scum formed a bathtub ring around her. "Why don't you introduce us, Ann?"

I glared up at her.

Lurlene said, "Hi. I'm Lurlene Brueggemeyer." She flashed her silver smile.

Jennifer proceeded to dump her tray of trash right into Lurlene's lap.

Gasping, Lurlene pushed back her chair and stood up.

My blood boiled. I reached over and picked up Lurlene's half-eaten corn dog. I dipped it in ketchup, then flung it at Jennifer. I think I only meant to spray her, but the dog flew off the stick and smacked her right in the forehead. The hot dog slid off, and a big glop of ketchup remained like a gunshot wound in her head.

Jennifer's hand flew up to her forehead. When she drew it back, it was smeared with ketchup. "I'm bleeding!" she screamed. "Oh, my God, I'm bleeding!" She pivoted on her Georgios and raced out of the cafeteria, her clique in tow.

"I hope you were through with that corn dog, Lurlene," I said.

Her shoulders began to shake. Tears filmed her eyes. Then she exploded in laughter. She let out a whoop that was about 8.5 on the Richter scale.

Her laugh was so infectious, I had to laugh, too. I even noticed other people around us laughing. Not too many, but a few.

When Kimberly didn't show up for school the next day, I should've called her. I didn't. Don't ask me why. Maybe I thought the separation would do our friendship some good. Meanwhile, Lurlene and I ate lunch together again at the corner table and practiced spelling. Lurlene even moved over into Kimberly's chair so the dictionary between us would be more convenient. I had a weird feeling about it. After all, that blue plastic chair had been Kimberly's for almost two years now. But come on. Nobody owns a cafeteria chair.

Before starting my lunch, I eagle-eyed for Jennifer Caldwell. She wasn't about to just forget something as hideous as a corn dog in the head. At her table she huddled with her masses, whispering and giggling. Plotting murder, no doubt.

"*Wrasse*," Lurlene said. " 'A brilliantly colored marine bony fish.' "

I turned my attention back to her. "Like bass, right? R-a-s-s."

She shook her head. "Not exactly. W-r-a-s-s-e," she spelled.

I clucked in disgust. "I thought we were in the *R*'s. No wait, the *S*'s."

"We are. It was a trick question. I was testing you on silent letters."

My look betrayed my lack of amusement.

"I'm sorry." Lurlene's face fell. "Don't get mad. It's the first one you've missed all week. You just weren't concentrating."

"I'm not mad. I can't get my mind on spelling today," I told her. "I think I burned up all my brain cells on that stupid history test this morning. Here, let me give you one." My search for a word was interrupted by someone coughing right behind me. Uh-oh. Here it comes.

"Kimberly, you're back!" I jumped up to greet her. "Have a seat."

In a thick, congested voice she said, "I would, but it looks like someone's taken my place." Before I could utter a word, she stormed out of the room.

I didn't see Kimberly the rest of the day, but I couldn't stop thinking about that look on her face. I called her as soon as I got home. She couldn't, or wouldn't, come to the phone. "She's resting," said Mrs. Hitler.

Yeah, right.

We always spent all our free time together during spelling season. It was a ritual. A way of life. Besides I was worried about her.

The next day I called after school, but no one answered. "She probably moved and forgot to mention it," I muttered to myself. Cursing under my breath, I punched in her number for about the bejillionth time.

"Hello?"

Shock. She was there. "I've been trying to call you for two days. Are you all right?"

"Yes. Why?" she asked coolly.

"You sounded really sick yesterday. I just wanted to explain about Lurlene."

"Don't bother."

"Kimberly, come on. Lurlene didn't mean to take your chair. We were just practicing spelling —" I stopped short. Open mouth, insert foot. "I'm sorry about your cold. Is there anything I can do?"

She didn't answer for a long, tense moment. Then, after a hack, she said, "Stop hanging around with her."

I didn't know what to say, so I said something stupid, of course. "I'm her sponsor. I can't."

"I think you're using that as an excuse, Ann. You know she doesn't need a sponsor anymore. Just between us, I can't stand her. She's totally annoying."

"She is not." The sharpness of my own voice surprised

me. I took a deep breath to calm myself. "You don't know her. She grows on you."

"Like a fungus. Look, it's either her or me. You decide." The phone clicked in my ear.

"That's not fair!" Unexpectedly, tears welled in my eyes. It *wasn't* fair. Kimberly had no right to force me to choose between her and Lurlene. Why couldn't she give Lurlene a chance? She knew if it came down to choosing, there wasn't really any choice. Was there?

The next day at school Lurlene was waiting for me at the front door. "Look, Ann," she said, all excited. "Look what I found in my locker." She thrust a note at me.

"What is it?" I unfolded the paper and started to read. "Dear Lurlene: I think you're the greatest-looking chick I've ever seen. I can't stop staring at you in class. I think I'm in love with you." It was signed, "Your Secret Admirer."

Lurlene beamed.

I seethed. What a dirty trick. Obviously the work of Jennifer Caldwell.

"I can't believe it," Lurlene breathed. "A secret admirer." She gingerly refolded the note and hugged it to her chest.

I placed a sympathetic hand on Lurlene's shoulder. "Lurlene, I don't really think —"

Just then Kimberly appeared. "So, is this your decision?" Her steely eyes fused onto mine.

I didn't get a chance to respond before Lurlene piped up, "Hi, Kimberly. Guess what?" She cupped a hand to Kimberly's ear. "I have a secret admirer."

Kimberly lurched back as if Lurlene were the human plague. "It's no secret," she snapped at me. "Her name is e-x-f-r-i-e-n-d."

"Kimberly, wait," I called, as she took off down the hall at warp speed. "Lurlene"— I whirled and rolled my eyes at her exasperatedly —"I need to talk to Kimberly. I'm sorry. I'll see you later, okay?"

She nodded. "Sure, okay."

I raced after Kimberly and caught up with her near the library. Grabbing her arm, I spun her around. "Hold it, Kimberly. It's not what you think."

She huffed. "Are we going to practice together at lunch?"

"Well, yeah. Of course."

"Alone?"

I gulped. "Sure. All right. Alone."

9

It took all morning to work up a plan — or maybe it was courage. After English I told Lurlene, "I'll probably be really late for lunch today. I have to do some research in the library for a, uh, a project in gym." Oh, lame, Ann. Like what? An essay on the history of hockey? Bull hockey. I continued, "It might be a good idea if you found another table to eat at. You know how bugged Kimberly gets when people bother her."

Lurlene held my shifting eyes, or tried to. "Especially me. When are we going to practice spelling again?"

"I don't know. But don't wait for me. You go ahead and practice on your own."

She sighed. "That's no fun. You let me know when you're free."

I felt my face catch fire and turned away. "I better get going," I mumbled before fleeing down the hall. Why did she have to be so nice?

I stalled around after gym to make sure I'd be really late to lunch. I figured I could sneak to the corner table without Lurlene noticing. Dumb, huh? When I rounded the corner, there she was. Like she was waiting for me.

"Ann, I was hoping to catch you. You wouldn't believe what just happened."

"Lurlene, you weren't supposed to wait for me, remember?"

"I wasn't waiting. I just got here. I'm sorry."

I wanted to scream.

"This really weird thing happened," she said. "I was coming down the hall, and all of a sudden people started saying hi to me. Not just one or two people. Everybody. It was so great. I didn't know if I'd ever fit in here, but now . . ." Her metal teeth sparkled at me. "Thank you. I don't know what you did. . . ."

Me neither, I thought as I smiled wanly. It really was weird. A girl with purple hair ambled by us on her way to the cafeteria. She stopped, backed up a couple of steps, and stared at Lurlene's back. Then she smirked and said, "Hey, Lurlene. Nice to meet ya."

Lurlene turned around. "Nice to meet you, too."

The girl almost somersaulted through the door, she was so doubled over with laughter.

"See?" Lurlene beamed.

I shook my head. I didn't get it.

"I'm starving," Lurlene said. "I wonder what's for lunch today. I hope McDonald's brought Big Macs." She headed for the doors. "Have a nice lunch. I won't bother you guys."

Then I saw it. "Lurlene, wait." I positioned myself directly behind her. A note was stuck on her back. In bold black letters it read, BE KIND TO GEEK WEEK. MY NAME'S LURLENE. I'M A GEEK. WON'T YOU SAY HI?

"Oh, Lurlene." I ripped the note off her back.

"What's that?" she asked.

"Nothing." I crumpled it up.

Before I could pitch it in the trash can, she plucked it out of my hand. As she read, her jaw began to quiver.

"Lurlene, it's just a stupid joke. Forget it."

Her hand fell to her side, and she let the note drop. Without warning, she tore off down the hall.

"Lurlene!" I raced after her.

She disappeared into the girls' rest room. By the time I got there, she'd already locked herself in a stall. Her sobs echoed off the tile as I slid down the wall to sit on the floor. "Lurlene, don't cry," I said. "It's just somebody's sick idea of a joke. Probably Jennifer Caldwell. She has a third-grade mentality, you know? Don't let her get to you."

After a few minutes of heart-wrenching sobs, the door

to Lurlene's stall creaked open. I scrambled to my feet. Lurlene came out, her face all blotchy red. I searched in my pack for a Kleenex and handed it to her.

"Why does everybody hate me?" she asked.

I took a deep breath. "They just don't know you. Not like I do. If people would give you a chance —"

"Why won't they?"

"Well . . ." I swallowed hard. "For one thing, you look kind of . . . different."

"You mean my braces? I hate them, too, but I can't help it if I have crooked teeth."

"It's not your braces, Lurlene. Not totally. I mean, well, let's start with your hair."

Lurlene glanced into the mirror over the sink. "I guess it is kind of messy." She removed a barrette, opened it with her teeth, and clamped it back at the nozzle end of her pigtail.

"In case you haven't noticed, Lurlene, no one wears their hair like that anymore. Braids are okay, and pony-tails in the back, but yours . . ." I trailed off.

Self-consciously, she wound a pigtail around her hand.

I plunged ahead. "And your clothes . . ."

She looked down at her flowered corduroy skirt and her boots. "What about them?"

"They're just kind of . . . old-fashioned." I met her eyes in the mirror. "It's not like clothes are that impor-tant to who you are inside. But, well, a lot of people

75

don't look any further." I dropped my eyes. Yeah, a lot of people.

Lurlene shook her head. "I don't know what to do. I want to fit in, but I don't know how. I mean, I can't do my hair in braids. I don't know how. And my mom makes all my clothes. I want people to like me. I don't want to be a . . . a geek." Tears filled her eyes again.

I slipped my arm around her waist. "You're not," I said.

"Yes, I am." She blew her nose on a paper towel. After a pause she said, "Would you help me? With my appearance at least?"

"Well, yeah, if you want me to."

Lurlene's face brightened. "I do."

"Hey, what's a sponsor for? Okay, first, we need to get your hair styled. I don't know how to French-braid either, but Kimberly —" Oops, bad idea. "Maybe they could show you at Hair Affair. That's where I get my hair cut. I have an idea, Lurlene. Why don't you come over tomorrow? It's Saturday. We could do a complete makeover on you. Before and after. Like on *Oprah*."

"On who?" Lurlene said.

"Never mind."

Lurlene forced a shaky smile. "Just don't make me over to look like Jennifer Caldwell, okay?"

I scoffed. "Who'd want to look like that ditz?"

10

A gully washer soaked the city Saturday morning. It was definitely springtime in the Rockies. Flash flood warnings went out all up and down the front range, including Denver. Lurlene showed up at my house around ten-thirty, looking like a drowned ferret. As I introduced her to Dad and Chase, they exchanged glances. "Geek," the look said. My return look warned, "Not one word or you're both dead meat."

"We're going to the mall, Dad," I informed him. "Could you loan me your Mastercard?"

"In your dreams," he muttered, and went back to reading his *Computerworld*.

"It's worth a try." I elbowed Lurlene. "How about an advance on my allowance. Say, the next year's worth?"

"You got that last week." Dad reached into his pocket. "Here's bus fare." He handed me a twenty.

Pure profit since I'd already bribed Chase to drive me to the Aurora Mall. I think Chase was having second thoughts, though, as he stood in the living room staring at Lurlene. Okay, she was a vision in her Agent Orange rain slicker. But he didn't have to stare.

Lurlene smiled at him. "Ann's going to degeek me."

Chase hyperventilated.

"Come on, let's go. We have a hair appointment at eleven."

We all piled into Chase's Geo. One little old lady was waiting to get her perm combed out when Lurlene and I splashed into Hair Affair a little after eleven. None of the stylists was busy, but we still had to wait. Why is that? We had an appointment. "I've never been to a beauty salon," Lurlene whispered. "What do I do?"

"Just tell the stylist what you want."

"What do I want?"

"Hmmm. Maybe I better go with you."

Lurlene's stylist was named Ginger. As in Ginger Snap. She wasn't much older than us, probably right out of beauty college. "So, what would you like today, Aileen?" she asked in her perky, high-pitched voice.

"Lurlene," I corrected since Lurlene was gagging from the plastic cape being Velcroed around her neck. Lurlene's bugged-out eyes pleaded with me.

"A cut and style," I told Ginger. "Not too short. Trim the split ends. I don't know, maybe bangs?" I tried to picture it.

Ginger removed the rubber bands and fluffed Lurlene's hair. "You have some natural curl," she stated the obvious. "I'd suggest, with your face . . ." Ginger studied Lurlene. Lurlene blushed a gusher. Ginger blinked mascara-caked eyelashes. "I'd go shoulder length with wispy bangs. Nothing heavy."

"Sounds good," I said.

"Let's go to the sinks." Ginger spun Lurlene around.

Lurlene freaked, like she was going to have to wash dishes or something.

"To get your hair washed," I informed her.

"Oh." Relief flooded her face.

Ginger combed and snipped and curled and blew Lurlene's hair dry. About forty-five minutes later, she spun Lurlene's chair all the way around and proclaimed, "Ta-da. What do you think, Colleen?"

Lurlene gazed into the mirror. A slow smile spread across her lips. "Wow," she said.

Standing behind her, I repeated the declaration. "Wow. You look terrific." She did, too. Like a normal person — from the neck up, anyway. Lurlene paid cash at the front desk, $22.50, "Plus a couple of dollars tip," I told her before she put the money away.

Out in the mall Lurlene refolded her wad of bills and

said, "It cost more than I thought. I only got fifty dollars out of my savings." Which left half of that for a whole new wardrobe. If you can buy a new wardrobe with twenty-five dollars, reveal your shopping secret.

We started at Young Deb and worked all the sales tables. Lurlene got a lemon yellow sweater and a blue jean skirt. Period. That would last her through Monday. Then what?

"Everything's so expensive," she said, while we waited in front of AMC theaters for Chase to pick us up.

"Tell me about it. At least me and Kimberly exchange clothes so we'll have some new outfits every year. We're not exactly the same size, but . . . hey!" That gave me an idea. Over Christmas Kimberly and I'd both gone through our closets and bagged a bunch of clothes. Not that they were ragged or worn-out; we'd just grown tired of them and needed the closet space for new stuff. The garbage bag was still in my garage waiting for our summer tag sale.

On the ride home, I explained to Lurlene about the clothes. It was tricky. I didn't want her to think they were charity. "You and Kimberly are just about the same height, too, so I bet her jeans will fit you. She grew out of all her best Guess last year."

"Who's best guess? About what?"

This kid was sheltered. "Never mind. You'll see."

"Gosh, Ann. No one's going to recognize me," Lurlene said, staring at her reflection in the rearview mirror.

Chase caught my eye. "What do you think of Lurlene's hair?" I asked him.

He shrugged. "It's hair. It grows on the head."

"Shut up."

"On the legs. In the pits."

I whapped him. Lurlene giggled. "Please," I warned her. "Don't encourage him."

At home, while I rummaged through the garbage bag, Lurlene perched on the edge of my bed. She studied herself in my bureau mirror. Every few seconds she flipped her hair. "Kimberly hates me, doesn't she?" Lurlene said out of the blue.

I paused and looked at her. "No, not really. She's just, I don't know, weird these days. I mean, she's usually telling *me* what a snob *I* am —" I stopped short. Hastily I added, "You must think she's really awful, Lurlene. But she's not. She's a nice person once you get to know her. At least the old Kimberly was. I'm not sure I even know this Kimberly. She's so obsessed with spelling and becoming champion of the world. I know she's under a lot of pressure, especially from her parents. Even so, it's not fair, you know? Why should I have to choose between you and her? I'm not going to drop *you* just because *she* doesn't want to ruin *her* reputation."

"What?" Lurlene's eyes grew wide. "She's making you choose?"

My eyes dug a trench in the carpet. I had such a big mouth.

Lurlene inhaled a long breath. "You don't have to choose between us. Kimberly's your best friend." She rose. "Maybe I should go."

I stood and pushed her back down. "No, Lurlene. It's not your fault. Kimberly and I'll work things out. She's just a mental case right now. After the spelling bee, things will change." I took my own deep breath and wondered, Will they? "Anyway, I can choose my own friends, thank you very much."

"Am I?"

"What? My friend? Of course you are." The realization hit hard. She was my friend. And I didn't care what anyone else thought.

Lurlene held my eyes. Her sudden metallic smile almost blinded me.

"Here, try on these white jeans and this silk blouse," I dumped them in her lap, "while I go get us something to eat. I'm having a major snack attack."

When I returned a few minutes later with a bag of Cheetos and two Diet Cokes, Lurlene was twirling in front of the mirror. "Perfect fit," she said, sucking in her stomach to snap the jeans. "Quick!" she wheezed. "Give me that Diet Coke."

Laughing, I handed it to her.

The turquoise blouse looked awesome. It was one Kimberly used to wear constantly, her very favorite until she ripped the seam on the sleeve. She must've fixed it, though, because I didn't see any gaping holes. As I studied Lurlene in the mirror, admiring herself, I thought, She doesn't look half bad. In fact, she looks three quarters good — if she'd only lose the cowboy boots.

11

On Monday while Lurlene and I were talking at my locker, Brad McKenzie showed up. "Hi, Ann," he said in that voice that makes me melt all over his Reeboks. He leaned up against the locker next to mine with his arm over my head. "Where's your geek?"

I cringed. Lurlene peeked out from behind me.

"Hi," Brad said. Just like that. "Hi."

"Hi," Lurlene said back.

"So where is she? I thought we should declare another geek week."

Two bolts of lightning struck me at once. First, he didn't even recognize Lurlene, and second, he was the one who initiated geek week.

"Who's your friend?" he asked, smiling at Lurlene.

She poked me in the back.

"This is Lurlene," I said coolly.

"You new here?"

Lurlene smiled shyly. "Sort of."

"You'll like it. Everyone's cool. Except maybe for the nerds." Brad rapped me on the head with a fist.

I pushed his arm away.

"Listen, Ann," he said. "If you see that geek, would you stick this note on her back? It was such a scream before. She really thought people were being nice to her." He snickered as he handed me the note.

I opened my mouth to reply but he cut me off. "By the way, Caldwell's having a party Friday night. If you're not busy, I thought maybe we could go together. I mean, I could lower myself just once for a nerrrd."

Brad McKenzie was actually asking me out. I'd been waiting for this moment all my life, I thought. Now, as I heard Lurlene shuffling books behind me and felt the weight of the ten-ton note in my hand, I balked. "What do you know about secret admirers, Brad?"

"Secret admirers? Oh, that." He chuckled. "That was Caldwell's idea. What a kill, huh?" He punched my arm. "So how about the party? I'll pick you up around seven?"

Suddenly I despised Brad McKenzie. Just like that. Hot to cold. "Sorry," I said. "I'm busy."

I tore the note into little pieces and let them sail to the floor at his feet. Grabbing Lurlene's sleeve, I brushed past a speechless Brad McKenzie. "Shut your mouth, Brad," I said. "You're attracting flies."

"What happened?" Lurlene asked, hustling to keep up with me as I stormed through the halls.

"Forget it. He's a jerk. I'm just glad I found out before I went out with him."

Lurlene stopped me. "I feel like I'm wrecking your whole life, Ann. Pretty soon you're not going to have any friends left." Her chin began to quiver.

"It's not your fault, Lurlene. And you're not wrecking my life. Some friends aren't worth keeping." My feet picked up speed. "And if it weren't for you," I said, stopping suddenly and pivoting, "I might never have found that out. Anyway, didn't you notice something else?"

She blinked back her tears.

I smiled at her. "He didn't recognize you. He thought you were new here."

"Hey, that's right."

In fact, no one in the hall stared or snickered. And during our morning classes a few people even said hi to Lurlene. During algebra Lurlene slipped me a note. "Isn't it funny how people treat me different just because I have new clothes?" it began. It ended, "I never realized how important looks are."

What could I say? It was snobbish and insensitive? That would be admitting *I* was snobbish and insensitive. Which I was.

At lunch we ran into Kimberly — literally. She was coming out the door as we were heading in. We just stared at each other without speaking. It was Lurlene who finally said, "Do you want to eat with us today, Kimberly?"

Kimberly blinked at her. "I switched to early lunch," she replied.

"You're eating with the seventh graders?" My voice rose an octave. "Are you that desperate to avoid us?" I don't think she heard me. She was surveying Lurlene up and down, up and down.

"Where did you get those clothes?" she asked in a strangled voice.

Lurlene flashed a wide smile at me. "Ann gave them to me. Along with a bunch of other outfits she didn't want anymore. Aren't they great?"

"Yeah. Great." Kimberly's magnified eyes bore into me so hard, I swear a machete slashed through my heart.

I blanched when I realized why. The turquoise blouse. "It's just that old stuff —"

"My old stuff." Kimberly clamped her jaw. As she wedged between us, I shivered from the ice crystals in the air.

There was a note waiting for me on Tuesday in study hall, a reminder that the Denver County spelling bee was scheduled for Friday morning, eight o'clock. It also reminded me that I hadn't yet talked to Mrs. Welter about getting Lurlene signed up. Immediately I asked Mr. Howell for a hall pass and went to the office.

Mrs. Welter's door was open a crack when I sat down to wait. I heard her say, "Tiffany, the dress code specifically states no halter tops. And I really don't think that earring in your nose is appropriate school wear, either."

Tiffany clucked audibly.

Mrs. Welter held the door for her. "You'll have to go home and change. And I expect you back here within the hour," she added to Tiffany's bare back.

Yeah, right, I thought. Beeline for the mall.

"Ann, you need to see me?" Mrs. Welter's voice sounded weary. I followed her in. "Sit." She motioned to a chair.

It was still warm from Tiffany's baked-on leather skirt.

"I saw Lurlene yesterday." Mrs. Welter's eyes brightened a bit. "She looks wonderful. What did you do to her?"

I blushed. "I just made a couple of clothes suggestions. Got her hair cut."

She smiled at me. "I knew I could count on you. How's she handling her parents' divorce?"

My eyes shifted over Mrs. Welter's shoulder to the dingy window behind her. "Not so good."

Mrs. Welter sighed. "It's tough. It's always hardest on the kids, and I'm not convinced they ever get over it. *I* know *I* didn't."

My eyes locked with hers, then dropped to the desk. I needed to change the subject fast. "I came to ask if Lurlene could go with us to the spelling bee on Friday," I said quickly.

She paused and considered. "I don't see why not. She'd probably enjoy watching you and Kimberly compete."

"No, I mean Lurlene should *enter* the spelling bee. She's great. No kidding, Mrs. Welter. She's as good a speller as Kimberly."

"Is she as good as you?" When her question was met with silence, she gave a short laugh and said, "Let me call over to the admin. building and get her name on the list, or whatever it is they do." She swirled through her Rolodex of phone numbers. "Here it is." After punching the numbers in, she spoke into the receiver, "Dr. Kinney, please. In Language Arts." She winked at me.

When he came on, she explained the situation. "Uh-huh," she said. "Uh-huh." She swiveled away from me in her chair. "I see," she mumbled. "You can't make an exception? Yes, uh-huh. Of course." She hung up.

A few seconds passed before she swiveled back to face me. "I'm sorry, Ann. It's too late," she said. "We can only send three spellers from each area. You, Kimberly, and the second-place winner who qualified."

Stephen somebody, from Horace Mann Middle School, I remembered.

Instead of going back to study hall, I locked myself

in a stall in the girls' rest room. I suspected Tiffany was next door. Tears stung my eyes. How was I going to tell Lurlene? She'd been working so hard, practicing every day and after school with me at the library when she could stay. I had her all psyched up, too, about acing the written test and going on to the orals. I really believed she had a chance to get that far. I think, too, that spelling took her mind off her rotten home life. She kept talking about going to Washington, D.C., and seeing her dad. Now she was in for a letdown. Another one. And it was my fault.

Lurlene asked me once during algebra if I was okay, that I looked a little pale. I just couldn't tell her. Not yet. "I'm fine," I lied. "Equivalent equations." I faked a gag.

She laughed. "I know what you mean."

After school I ambled aimlessly toward the library. I had to tell her, I just had to. But how? See, it's like this, Lurlene, I practiced a mental monologue. I screwed up. Royally. You're going to hate me. You're never going to trust me again. I didn't mean to get your hopes up. Really —

A familiar voice cut through my rehearsal: "Ann, wait up."

It was Kimberly. "Mind if I talk to you?" she said.

I shrugged. "Sure you want to associate with a lower life form?"

She stiffened.

"That was mean," I said. "I'm sorry."

She sat down on a bench with me outside the media center. "That's okay. I deserved it."

Shock. Had the old Kimberly at long last returned? Our eyes met in a flicker of recognition. "So, how are you?" I asked.

"Nervous about Friday. How about you?"

I held up a trembling hand. I didn't even have to fake it.

"I know you guys have been working hard. I've seen you. Is Lurlene as good as I think she is?"

My eyebrows arched. "She is good, Kimberly. But you don't have to worry about Lurlene." I do.

"What about you?" Kimberly said. "You still planning to beat me this year?"

I laughed wryly. "Sure, Kimberly. Just like last year and the year before. You're probably quaking in your boots. And if you don't have any boots, maybe Lurlene could loan you a pair."

She choked on a laugh.

I smiled back and shook my head. "You know, she really is a neat person once you get to know her."

Kimberly blinked and looked away.

"Hi, Kimberly. Hi, Ann. Sorry I'm late. I had to finish

that homework assignment for English so we could practice spelling tonight." Lurlene flopped down beside me.

Kimberly's lips grew taut.

"You want to practice with us?" Lurlene asked her, peering around me. "We're down to the Z's. You can keep us awake when we start to"— she lolled her head back and snored — "catch our z's." Lurlene giggled at her own joke.

Kimberly replied in a flat voice, "I can't. I just stopped by to wish you good luck." She stood and met my eyes, not Lurlene's.

I didn't reply.

It was Lurlene who said, "Good luck to you, too, Kimberly. Break a leg. Not really."

"You, too," Kimberly muttered. Under her breath she added, "Really."

12

"I have to be home by six tonight," Lurlene said as we settled in to a study carrel near the PCs in the library. "Mom's taking a night class to bone up on her skills." Lurlene elbowed me. "Get it? Bone up?"

I curled a lip. "Did you tell *her* to break a leg?"

Lurlene howled.

"Shhh," the librarian scolded.

It was time. "Maybe we could just skip spelling tonight," I said, dropping my head into my arms on the desk. "I'm pretty beat."

"Are you zapped, zonked, or zoned out?" Lurlene said as she opened the dictionary to the Z's.

"Zombied. With a capital Z."

"There aren't too many Z's." Lurlene counted the pages.

"We could probably get through them tomorrow at lunch — if we zoom."

"Lurlene . . ."

She glanced at the clock behind us. "Since we're not going to spell, I really should go home," she cut me off. "There's a lot to do around the house with Mom working and stuff. Do you mind?"

"Uh, no, not at all." I hoped I didn't sound too anxious to see her go.

She repacked her stuff. At the door she waved and said, "Zee you tomorrow, Ann."

I smiled somberly and watched her leave. Maybe by then I'd have thought of a way to break the news without breaking apart our friendship.

All night I lay in bed trying to think of a way to get Lurlene into the spelling bee. She deserved to go; she was an awesome speller. Maybe not as good as Kimberly, but a lot better than me. If only it wasn't our last year, our last chance.

A sigh escaped my lips. Not that I had a chance, but I'd never won anything in my life. Second place, yeah, lots of times in spelling. Third on the balance beam once in sixth grade. Fourth in a short story contest. But never first. Not like Kimberly. She won first in everything she tried. Her parents were there for her, always, because she was number one.

Why was I thinking about her parents? I wondered. Because mine had deserted me? Yeah, I guess that's how I felt. Especially Mom. She used to drill me on the practice booklets. She used to be involved in my life, in everything I did. Now it seemed so different between us, so strange. When we talked on the phone, it was as if we were total strangers. And it wasn't much better at her apartment. Man, I hated this divorce.

"Back to the real issue, Ann," I rearranged my priorities out loud. "Spelling. Maybe Kimberly needs a little competition to get her nose out of the air." I laughed. Right. Like *I'd* be a serious threat. Then it struck me, *clunk*, like a dictionary dropped on my head. There was a way to get Lurlene in. But it meant . . . no, forget it.

Selfish, I scolded myself. That's what you are. Lurlene has a real chance to make it to the state finals, and you have to give her that chance.

The next day I resumed our normal spelling routine with Lurlene. I didn't want her to get suspicious of my plan, because I knew she'd never go along with it. By the end of lunch, we'd finished the dictionary and started back through the practice booklets. "We'll concentrate on the words with silent letters," I told Lurlene on the way to study hall, "since that seems to be your weakness."

"You don't have a weakness, do you?" she said.

"Nope, not-a-one. Unless you count foreign words,

medical terms, silent letters, and any word with more than one syllable."

She laughed.

I didn't.

On Thursday morning I woke up with a sick feeling. Today, Ann Keller would become a sacrificial lamb. Chase always said I was the black sheep of the family, and I was about to prove him right. Overnight I'd developed a terminal case of the cold. It wasn't out of the question that I could've picked up Kimberly's virus. Mrs. Welter would have to send Lurlene to the spelling bee in my place. I was just too sick. Hear me cough? "Hack, hack."

"You don't sound so good," Lurlene said after I hacked my head off in history. By lunchtime she was really worried. "Let me feel your forehead." She slid a cool palm under my bangs.

Burn, baby, burn, I commanded my skin.

"You don't have a fever."

So much for biofeedback. I faked a sneeze. "I don't know if I'm going to be able to go tomorrow," I said in my most nasal drone.

"What?" Lurlene's eyes grew as wide as Frisbees. "You have to go. You'll be okay. You're just stressed out. You need to go home and rest."

At that moment a shadow cooled our table. "Ann, I need to talk to you." Mrs. Welter rapped the table with her knuckles. Whoa, it must be an emergency, I thought. Mrs. Welter coming into the cafeteria? That's why the din had dropped dramatically. "You, too, Lurlene."

"What'd we do?" Lurlene whispered as we trailed her out the double doors.

"Got me." But it couldn't be good.

"Close the door," Mrs. Welter said when we arrived in her office. I eased the door shut. "Sit," she commanded. We obeyed.

"I've been working on this spelling bee dilemma, trying to find some way to get Lurlene into the contest."

"Huh?" Lurlene frowned.

I coughed. "Mrs. Welter, it's, it's not a problem anymore." I hacked into my fist.

She ignored me. "Finally it came to me. Lurlene can claim she's home schooled. I called and checked. Home schoolers can sign up for the spelling bee at any time, up to the day of the state competition. I know it isn't exactly the truth." In a conspiratorial voice she added, "We'll just keep it between the three of us."

For a prolonged moment, no one spoke. Inwardly I rejoiced. Rejoiced and cured the common cold. Joy! I could go. We could all go.

Lurlene spoke up, "So, tomorrow at the spelling bee, I'm supposed to tell them I'm home schooled?"

"They'll add your name to the list of spellers at the registration table," Mrs. Welter said. "Don't worry. I'll be there to vouch for you. Does anyone need a ride uptown? Lurlene?"

"No," I answered for her. "We're going together."

Lurlene turned her head slowly and looked at me. "No, we're not," she said.

"We're not?"

Lurlene blinked and then met Mrs. Welter's eyes. "I can't do it," she said. "I can't lie."

13

After Lurlene rushed out of the principal's office, she disappeared. I didn't see her at all the rest of the day, and she wasn't waiting for me at the library after school, either. By the time I got home, I was frantic and called her. "You have to go, Lurlene," I said when she answered the phone. "You're a great speller, and it's your only chance to compete. Eighth grade is the last year."

"Why didn't you tell me the truth?" she said. "That I couldn't compete?"

I explained the situation, about qualifying and all.

After a pause Lurlene said, "So you were going to let me go in your place?"

"You're a much better speller than me, Lurlene. You'd have a good chance against Kimberly. Against everyone else —"

"No." She cut me off. "I can't lie. I won't."

"It's not really a lie. I mean, you *were* in home school when the elimination rounds were going on. You couldn't have competed. Besides, you weren't even living in this state!"

Lurlene didn't answer for a long time. When she did, her voice was shaky. "I wish we'd never come here. I wish I *was* back in home school. Why can't things be the way they were? Why?" Before I could answer, she hung up.

I felt worse than a worm. Some friend I was. Some sponsor. Now Lurlene hated school. She hated school and she hated me. So did Kimberly. At that moment I wasn't too crazy about myself.

The next morning Dad drove me to East High School, where the Denver County spelling bee was being held this year. I'd never gone to a spelling bee alone. Kimberly and I had always ridden together, every year. Even though Dad was chipper as a chipmunk, he couldn't pull me out of my blue funk. In the parking lot, he reached over and patted my knee. "Don't worry so much, Annie," he said. "You'll do grrrreat."

He didn't understand. He couldn't.

When we walked in, Mrs. Welter was already there talking to Mr. and Mrs. Tyne. Dad stopped just inside the door, squeezed my shoulder, and said, "I'm sorry, honey. I can't stay."

"What!"

"Work, you know." He grimaced. "Good luck. Spell well." He bent down and kissed my cheek.

My eyes followed him out to the car. "Kimberly's dad's here," I muttered at his back. "He gave up work to come. It was important enough for *him*."

I shrugged off my disappointment, or tried to. Mrs. Welter waved to me. Then an extraordinary thing happened. The front door whooshed open, and in clomped Lurlene.

I rushed over to her. "You came after all."

Lurlene clutched her spelling notebook to her chest. "Mom and I had a long talk. She convinced me it was an opportunity I shouldn't pass up."

See, that's what moms are for, I thought. Wish I had one.

I was so happy to see Lurlene that I threw my arms around her, right there in public.

"I'm still not sure I'm doing the right thing," she said.

"You are."

"I hope I don't go to hell for lying."

"If you do, I'll meet you at the gates," I said.

That made her laugh. As we meandered over to join Mrs. Welter and the Tynes, Lurlene looked around. "Are all these people spellers?" she asked.

"Most of them. I think they split us into eight or ten areas, with three spellers from each area. The private schools send a bunch. Plus all the home schoolers." I wiggled my eyebrows at her. "Wait till you see state."

"You really think we can beat all these people?"

"No."

She gave me a funny look.

"*We* can't. But *you* can. You're a fantastic speller."

Suddenly her face turned a sickly shade of green. I thought she was going to demonstrate the definition of *regurgitate*.

"Relax, Lurlene. You'll do great." I squeezed her hand to calm her.

During check-in, I saw Lurlene cross her fingers behind her back when she identified herself as a home schooler. Afterward, she ran to the rest room and kept running back about a hundred times. While I was sticking on my name tag, Kimberly came up beside me.

"Have you seen my father?" she asked. "He was supposed to drill me before the test." She scanned the gymnasium with her binocular eyes.

"No." A snide remark came to mind, but I shot it down. "What room are you in?"

She glanced at her registration card. "Room 201. Where are you?"

"Room 203. I think Lurlene's in 201 with you. She's a basket case. You nervous?"

Her eyes met mine, and she swallowed hard. "Yes. Are you?"

"I don't really have a chance. I'm more nervous for you and Lurlene."

Kimberly frowned. "Ann, I think you have a good chance. Despite what you think, I've always said you were a great speller."

When? I wondered. You never said it to me.

"In fact, when you told me you were going to beat me this year, I was scared. I mean, you probably could if you put your mind to it."

Was she kidding? I'm sure my chin hit the floor and bounced to the ceiling.

"Hi, Kimberly. Ann, does my hair look all right? Is this where my name tag goes? It probably won't stay stuck on this silky blouse. I shouldn't have worn this outfit. I'll probably sweat, and everyone will notice my armpits. What time is it? Do I have time to call my mom? I have to go to the bathroom again."

"Nerves of steel," I said as we watched Lurlene charge the girls' room.

Kimberly laughed. She actually laughed at my joke.

The county spelling bee was different this year — just a written test of two hundred words. No oral, which was a relief for everyone, I'm sure. Except the adults, but they didn't have to get up there and humiliate themselves. Although ribbons were awarded for tenth place on up, only the top three spellers would advance to state.

The test began with an easy word, *chic*. I wondered if Lurlene knew it. It wasn't one of the words we'd practiced, since it was so common, splashed all over *Seventeen* magazine every month. She probably never heard of *Seventeen*. If she mistook it for the homophone, she might write s-h-e-i-k.

The next word was *quinquagenary*. Long, but spelled phonetically. Lurlene shouldn't have any trouble with it. *Psychosis*. If she remembered the silent letter at the beginning, she should get that one, too.

The last word was finally pronounced, and it was easy. But after an hour of mental strain, my concentration waned.

I could not for the life of me remember how to spell *dyslexia*.

Was it *disleksia*? No, cross that out. *Disleczia*? That didn't look right. *Dizlexya? Disleksea? Dizlexheehaw?* Finally, eyes crossed, I settled on *dysleksia*. I knew before I dotted the *i* that it was wrong.

By the time our room let out, spellers were already packing the gymnasium discussing the test. I searched the bleachers for Lurlene. No sign of her, but I did spy Mrs. Welter with Kimberly's parents. Reluctantly I stepped up the risers to join them.

"Ann, how was it?" Mrs. Welter scootched over, giving me no choice but to squeeze between her and Mrs. Tyne.

"Not bad. There was only one word I was unsure about, but knowing Lurlene, she'll probably get it right."

Mrs. Tyne made a guttural noise in her throat.

"I'm sure Kimberly got them all," I added quickly.

Just then Kimberly climbed up the bleachers, followed close behind by Lurlene. I escaped to sit with Lurlene on the riser below, while Kimberly moved in between her parents. "Tell us every word and how you spelled it," I heard her mother say.

"Tyrant," I muttered. Lurlene was awfully quiet. "How'd you do?" I whispered.

She shook her head. What did that mean?

"How do you spell *chic?*" she said. "C-h-e-e-k?"

I groaned.

She turned to me and grinned. "Just kidding."

I elbowed her in the ribs.

It took about a year to grade the tests. We spent the time fidgeting, bounding up and down the bleachers, wandering to the rest room, outside, inside.

Finally the announcer stepped up to the crackly microphone. "Testing, tes . . ." The microphone died, then "*Testing,*" it exploded eardrums. "People, if you will please . . ." Dead. "*With your school.*" Squinch.

"Mrs. Barbara 'Bunny' Mertz, the school board president, will present the awards to our top spellers," the announcer said. "I'd like to take this opportunity to congratulate each and every one of you for your outstanding achievement in spelling. We recognize the many hours you've spent preparing for this competition, and we salute your efforts." Teachers, parents, and principals filled the gymnasium with applause.

Okay, Bunny, hop to it, I thought.

". . . And let me say further that the *Rocky Mountain News,* our sponsor, in partnership with the schools . . ." People were drifting off. The bleachers were beginning to rock with impatient foot stomping.

Bunny finally smoothed the results list against the lectern. Into the mike she said, "Okay, here we go. In tenth place, Mary Borodin from Smiley Junior High." The audience burst into applause. "Mary, come up for your ribbon."

The ceremony progressed ever so slowly. With each new announcement, everyone sucked in a collective breath.

"Fifth place with a score of ninety-seven, Joseph Miller from Holy Family Academy. Joseph, congratulations."

My bottom was getting stiff. My hands were sweating. When I rotated my head around to stretch my neck, I caught Kimberly's eye. She was leaning forward, elbows on knees, chin on fists. She crossed her eyes at me.

"In fourth place, scoring ninety-eight percent, Ann Marie Keller from Shiffley Middle School." My neck broke from whiplash. Everyone bounded to their feet, screaming, "Get up! Get up! Go get your ribbon!"

Lurlene squeezed my hand, tears filling her eyes.

"Congratulations, Ann Marie. Excellent work." Bunny handed me a ribbon and shook my trembling hand. I tromped back up the bleachers, hugging the prize to my chest.

"Let me see," Lurlene said. She took the ribbon from me and held it up for everyone to see. The white silk was embossed with gold lettering: FOURTH PLACE, DENVER COUNTY SPELLING BEE.

"Fantastic!" Mrs. Welter patted my shoulder.

Fighting back the tears, I tried to listen to the announcer. I pretended they were tears of joy. Problem was, fourth place didn't advance to state.

14

I just assumed I'd be going to the state competition. Last year I qualified and the year before. It never occurred to me I'd be eliminated this early on. Ever since I started competing in the spelling bees in third grade, I'd dreamed of becoming the National Spelling Bee champion.

Dream on, Ann.

In my despondency, I missed the name of the third place winner. Then, "It seems we have a tie for first and second place," Bunny said. "Wait a minute. Is this right?" She backed away from the mike and consulted with the announcer. "Yes, it's a new record," she said when she came back on. "Two spellers both scored one hundred percent on the test."

Cheers rang out from the crowd.

Bunny continued, "From Shiffley Middle School, Kimberly Tyne, and from home school, Lurlene Brueggemeyer."

Like slow-motion replay, we rose to our feet in unison. Kimberly was cool. Lurlene looked and shook like lime Jell-O.

My bottom lip quivered as I watched my friends accept the blue ribbon, along with the standing ovation from the crowd. Since there was only one ribbon, they'd have to share. That'll be interesting, I thought. No doubt the Tynes had already cleared a spot for it in their trophy case.

Behind me I heard Mrs. Tyne say, "That girl is *not* in home school. She goes to Shiffley with Ann and Kimberly."

Uh-oh. Trouble with a capital *T*.

I caught up with Kimberly on the way out. Everyone was stopping to congratulate her and wish her good luck in the state competition.

"Good going, Kimberly. I knew you could do it," I said. "Champion of the world, right?"

She narrowed her eyes at me.

"I didn't mean it like that," I apologized. "If you'd like me to help you practice for state —"

Her mother grabbed her by the arm. "I think we can handle it ourselves," she said to me coolly. "Come along, darling. I need to speak to Bunny."

My cheeks flared. Kimberly looked totally humiliated.

Mrs. Welter appeared out of the crowd, calling back, "Kimberly, congratulations again. Now where's that Lurlene?"

I spotted Lurlene coming out of the rest room. "I'll get her," I said. By the drinking fountain I grabbed her arm and whispered, "If anyone asks, you've been in home school all your life. You never heard of public school."

She gave me a funny look. Then beaming, she added, "Oh, Ann, I can't believe this. I've never won anything in my life. I couldn't have done it without you."

I shook my head. "You did it all on your own, Lurlene. If you want, I'll help you practice for state."

"We'll help each other." Lurlene smiled.

"Lurlene," I informed her, "I'm eliminated. Fourth place goes no place. Remember?"

She deflated visibly. Her eyes took on a sadness I'd never seen before. "But you have to go, Ann. I don't want to go without you."

Over the next month, every minute of my spare time was devoted to coaching Lurlene. Since I wasn't going to compete, I was going to make sure she spelled well. For once, I really was going to act like her sponsor. We met at my locker in the mornings, spelled on our way to class, between classes, during lunch. Even with all that practicing, by the end of the first week I knew we were in trouble.

"It's not enough, Lurlene," I told her. "We're only up

to the *BL*'s, and we barely have three weeks until state. Somehow we're just going to have to find more time." I chomped into my Taco Bell Taco Supreme.

Lurlene set down her milk and sighed. "Maybe we could go a little faster during lunch. I mean, if we really pushed . . ."

"We'll never make it. Why don't you come to my house after dinner every night, and we can practice until nine or ten."

She shook her head. "My mom's hours changed. She's working the third shift at the hospital, and I have to baby-sit until eight, sometimes nine o'clock, when the boys go to bed."

"Then we'll practice at your house."

"M-my house?" she stammered.

"Sure, while you baby-sit."

"It's kind of noisy," she said.

"It'd be better than nothing. I really think we have to. Don't you?"

Between her fingers she measured the dictionary pages that were left, then smiled grimly.

"Here, write down your address, and call me after school. I'll have Chase bring me over, if it's okay with your mom." I passed her my notebook.

It took a minute before she started writing. Why was she so hesitant to have me come over? Was she embarrassed by me? Didn't her mother approve of me as a friend? It'd been known to happen. Suddenly I felt kind of . . . geeky. Thankfully, Lurlene called me after school with the go-ahead.

I had to blackmail Chase to take me to Lurlene's. The cigarette butt I found in his backseat ashtray worked like a charm. At Lurlene's, Chase waited in the car until somebody answered the door for me. I thought that was considerate, until he squealed away from the curb like the hot dog he was.

"Hi, Ann. Come on in." Lurlene kicked a stuffed moose out from under the door. "We can practice in my room."

"What?" I shouted.

"In my room," she shouted back. "Finish your dinner and pick up the plates!" she hollered to no one in particular. In a calmer voice she said, "You've met my brothers." She mumbled the names again so fast I didn't catch them, plus the commotion of a stampede of screaming meemies through the house was kind of distracting.

Lurlene gestured me to follow her across the living room toward a hallway in the back. It was a treacherous journey. We had to step over books and clothes and sleeping dogs and rubber snakes — I think they were rubber — and half-eaten plates of spaghetti.

Lurlene led me to her bedroom and shut the door. "Like I said, it's kind of noisy here." She kicked a skirt out of the way to make a path. "Make yourself at home."

I flopped on her bed, then jumped up to peel a hairbrush from my seat.

Lurlene blushed. "I, uh, didn't have time to clean up my room. Sorry."

I smiled. "That's okay. You should see mine."

"I have. It's gorgeous. In fact, your whole house is beautiful. I'm really embarrassed to have you come over here." She started tossing clothes into the closet.

"Don't be," I said. "It's kind of homey." And I wasn't just being tactful. It felt comfortable. A lot more inviting than Kimberly's sterilized and sanitized mausoleum. I mean, you couldn't even put your feet on the furniture there. I kicked off my shoes and sprawled across the bed. One of Lurlene's brothers opened the door, screamed, and slammed the door. "*Boisterous*," I said. " 'Marked by or expressive of exuberance and high spirits.' Sentence: Your brothers are boisterous."

Lurlene rolled her eyes. "That's an understatement."

The next two weeks shot by. Mom called during spring break to ask if Chase and I wanted to come spend the week with her. "I miss you," she said. She sounded sad.

"Miss you, too, Mom. But I really need to help Lurlene practice for the spelling bee."

"Lurlene. Have I met her?"

"No. She's new this year."

"What happened to Kimberly?"

Good question. "She's possessed," I said. "I don't know. It's like this spelling bee has taken over her whole life. You know how her parents are. I think she inherited their perfection gene —"

"I'm sorry, honey. I just noticed the time. I have to run. House to show. Why don't you give me a call tomorrow and we'll talk about it."

Sure, I thought. If you remember we even had this conversation.

On the last Friday night before the spelling bee, Lurlene and I were in her room, trying like mad to get through the dictionary. At least I was.

"What should I wear to the spelling bee tomorrow, Ann?" Lurlene asked. She was sorting through the clothes in her closet as I frantically scanned the last page of W's.

"*Wrong, wrongful, wrongheaded.* Here's one. VUN-der-kint. *Wunderkind:* 'a child prodigy; one who succeeds in a competitive or highly difficult field or profession at an early age.' I'd say you qualify." I looked up at her.

"What about this red skirt? I've been saving it for a special occasion."

Like a fire sale? I didn't say it.

"Sure, that's fine. But we'd better cram. We still have the Y's and Z's to go and it's already"— I glanced at my watch —"nine fifty-five? Chase'll be here any minute."

"I could wear my old boots with it. They're a little

114

small, but they have red stars on the toes. Would that look okay?"

"YAB-ber. To talk, jabber."

"I could put a red bow in my hair and wear red tights. I have lots of red stuff."

"Lurlene?"

"Huh?"

"Spell *yabber.*"

She stretched to the ceiling and yawned. "I can't spell anymore tonight. Let's quit. I'll get up early tomorrow morning and finish."

"Promise? I could stay as late as you want to help you get done."

Lurlene shook her head. "You've done enough. Oh, that reminds me." She scrounged around in the junk on top of her dresser and handed me a small box. "This is for you."

I stuck my arm through my jacket sleeve, took the box, and turned it over in my hand. It was wrapped in Snoopy Christmas paper. "It's a little early for Christmas, isn't it? And my birthday's not until September."

"It's just a little present for helping me so much. For being my sponsor and coach. I just wanted you to know how much I appreciate it. And how special I think you are."

I swallowed the rising lump in my throat. "Thanks. But I didn't really do anything."

115

"Yeah, right." She folded her arms. "You degeeked me." She smiled. "Come on. Open it."

I tore into the wrapping, then sliced with a fingernail through the masking tape that secured the box lid. Inside, under a layer of toilet paper, was a delicate little brooch. It was gorgeous, ivory with a pink cameo in the middle. I lifted it out.

"It belonged to my grandmother," Lurlene said. "She gave it to me on my eleventh birthday, right before she . . . she died. She said it was a friendship pin that her best friend gave her when they were girls. She said one day I'd find a friend to pass it on to. Someone I wanted to be friends with forever."

Now I had a lump the size of a meatball in my throat. I couldn't force it down for the life of me.

"Would you put it on?" I said in a strangled voice. "Right here." I opened my coat and pressed a spot over my heart.

She pinned the brooch on my shirt, studied her work, and repinned it. Then she stood back and smiled a huge, warm smile.

"Thanks, Lurlene." I felt a tear roll down my cheek. I hated to cry in front of people. I hugged her awkwardly before rushing out the door.

15

I don't know why, but I expected Kimberly to call me the morning of the spelling bee. Last year we'd driven into downtown Denver together in her dad's new Saab, I remember. Of course her parents had drilled her the whole way, while in the backseat we'd made up wacky sentences for the words and laughed like hyenas. I missed Kimberly. The old Kimberly.

Lurlene's mom had taken the day off to go to the spelling bee, and she and Lurlene were driving to Currigan Hall together. Lurlene asked me to come along, but I knew she rarely got to spend time alone with her mom, so I said no, I'd already made other plans.

"I can't believe you dragged me out of bed for this," Chase grumbled all the way downtown.

"Well, Dad had an early morning meeting he couldn't reschedule," I muttered. "Or so he said."

Chase exhaled a long breath. "Okay, but this is it, Ann. The last time I ever take you anywhere. You've gotten enough mileage out of that cigarette butt. How long is this thing, anyway? When can I leave?"

"It usually lasts all day."

He moaned. "I have practice at four, so we have to split by three. Why are you going, anyway? You're not spelling."

"Rub it in."

He blinked at me. "I'm sorry. I didn't mean —"

"I just want to be there for Lurlene, okay?"

We didn't speak the rest of the way. I guess he understood about being there for someone else.

Hundreds of spellers were lining up in front of the registration table when we walked in. As if drawn by a magnet, my eyes fixed on the stage, where the oral competition would take place later that afternoon.

The judges' table was stationed on the left side of the stage, dictionaries poised. Two TV cameras had been set up at each end. In the middle of the stage, rising from the floor, stood the slender steel rod of the spellers' microphone.

Before I heard Lurlene call out to me, I saw red. "Oh,

no," I gasped. "I should've helped her pick out something to wear. Something not quite so . . . r-e-d."

"Ann! Over here. I have seats saved."

Under his breath Chase said, "I'm not with you. I don't know you —"

"Shut up." I grabbed him and dragged him down the aisle to a half-filled row of metal chairs.

"Hi, Chase," Lurlene said, flashing a smile at him.

"Hi," he growled before sprawling in a seat.

Kimberly and her parents sat a few rows ahead of us. Mrs. Tyne smoothed Kimberly's hair while Mr. Tyne drilled her from this year's "Words of the Champions" practice booklet.

"Oh, Ann. I wish you were spelling with me today," Lurlene said in a sigh.

I inhaled deeply. "Me, too. But you can win, Lurlene," I said. "Just don't lose your cool. And remember the silent letters."

"I'm so nervous." She began to shake her hands as if they were on fire.

"Calm down, Lurlene." I folded her hands between mine.

Suddenly a voice cut through the crowd noise. "Ann! I'm so glad you're here." I turned around.

"Hurry. You only have a few minutes." Mrs. Welter pulled me to my feet.

"W-what's going on?" I stammered.

"The third place winner had an appendicitis attack last night. He's in the hospital. You're the alternate, Ann. You need to get registered. Hurry!"

My eyes bugged right out of my head, I'm sure. Lurlene began to cheer. Chase got up and shoved me toward the registration table. And when I glanced over my shoulder, he and Lurlene were high-fiving each other.

The state competition began with a written test — one hundred words. Only the top twenty-five spellers would advance to the orals.

The first few words were easy: *vampire, bonanza, talc.* The next group I'd classify as intermediate, only because they were long. *Nasturtium, rumormonger, medicolegal.* That was just a warm-up. Next came *graminivorous, dissymmetry, otorhinolaryngology.* Aargh.

Many of the spellers requested repronunciations, repeats of sentences. I wrote and wrote and crossed out and rewrote. At the end I figured I got about six right.

We filed back to the auditorium after the test to wait for the results. Kimberly sat with her parents while Lurlene and I hung around the refreshment table, nibbling cookies.

Around noon a speaker announced that the grading was taking longer than expected and suggested we all break for lunch. Accompanied by Lurlene and her mom, Chase and I wandered down to Larimer Square. Even though my stomach was a butterfly breeding ground, I managed to choke down a burger at the Tabor Center food court.

When we returned a little after one, the list of words was posted. But not the names of the winners.

I started to scan the list when I noticed Kimberly beside me. "How'd you do?" I asked as we both read through the words. She moaned. She must've missed one.

"I almost called you to drive down with us today," she said.

"Why didn't you?"

She shrugged. "I assumed you were coming with Lurlene."

"I didn't."

"You didn't?" Our eyes locked. She pushed her glasses up her nose.

"My mom tried to get her thrown out of the competition, you know."

I'd forgotten all about that. "What happened?"

Kimberly said, "We had a real knock-down-drag-out about it. I mean, Lurlene proved herself at the spelling bee. She has a right to be here today, as much right as I do. Or anyone else."

Was this Kimberly Decimate-the-Competition Tyne?

"Besides, she's your friend," Kimberly added. "Lurlene never was the one I was worried about."

Before I could ask who was, a shout rang out from the

crowd. We turned to witness a group of official-looking people mounting the steps to the stage.

"Good luck, Kimberly," I whispered automatically, squeezing her arm.

"You, too," she said.

"There you are, Annie. How'd you do?"

"Dad!"

He stood at the end of my row.

"And Mom! What are you guys doing here?"

Dad said, "Chase called me." He looked at Mom.

"He called me, too," she said. "He told me you got to the spelling bee and made it to the finals, so I got here as fast as I could."

My eyes searched out Chase in the chairs. He sneered. I sneered back. Liar, I mouthed.

The speaker's voice reverberated from the stage, "Ladies and gentlemen. If you'll please take your seats, we're ready to announce the twenty-five spellers who will advance to the oral spelling bee."

Mom went in first and sat on my left while Dad sat on my right. I peered around Mom and Chase to catch Lurlene's eye. Green Lurlene. She looked like Christmas now.

"As I read each name and school, will the competitor please come to the judges' table for a number? Tie on the number vest and take a seat to my left. And spellers, please remain seated onstage in numerical order."

The auditorium buzzed. The announcer quipped, "The names are not in alphabetical order. Just to keep you in suspense."

Chase and I exchanged grimaces. Sick adult humor, I thought.

"Number one. Michael Nesbitt from Orion Junior High in Lakewood, Colorado." A group at the back rose to their feet, cheering him on as Michael walked up the aisle to receive his number.

"Number two . . ."

Kimberly was number four, and we cheered her to competitors' row. I glanced over. Lurlene worried the lace on her dress until I thought the hem would unravel.

Chase leaned over and said to me, "You're next."

I clucked. "Get real."

"Number twenty-one. Lurlene Brueggemeyer. Home school in Denver."

Our whole row stood in unison to applaud as Lurlene threaded her way down the row toward the aisle.

"I just know she's going to win," I said out loud to no one in particular. Kimberly's parents heard me, though. They turned in their chairs to glare.

"Number twenty-two. Ann Marie Keller. Shiffley Middle School.

I catapulted out of my seat. "I made the orals!" I yelled. Mom and Dad hugged me in turn. As I slipped on my number vest, I glanced down from the stage. Mom and Dad had moved together in the row, and they were laughing, together! It was the happiest moment of my life.

16

Rules were strict during the oral competition. The pronouncer would give each speller a word, then use it in a sentence. Spellers were allowed to ask for definitions, derivations, and alternate pronunciations.

The first speller approached the microphone. "Michael Nesbitt from Lakewood. How are you, Michael?" the pronouncer asked.

"Fine," he said tentatively into the microphone. I knew he was about as fine as limp spaghetti.

"Your word is DIS-truh-fee. *Dystrophy*. Muscular dystrophy is thought to be a genetic disorder and currently has no cure. *Dystrophy*."

"*Dystrophy*. May I have the derivation?"

The judges conferred. "New Latin."

"*Dystrophy. Dystrophy.*" He was using a well-worn stall tactic. Pronounce the word a hundred times. "*Dystrophy. Dystrophy.* Dis-TRO-fee?"

The pronouncer studied his sheet. "No. DIS-truh-fee."

"*Dystrophy. Dystrophy.*"

Get on with it, I muttered to myself.

"*Dystrophy.* D-y-s-t-r-o-p-h-y. *Dystrophy.*"

"Correct."

We all exhaled. The audience applauded.

"Please hold your applause until a contestant spells out," the pronouncer said. He moved on to speller number two.

Kimberly drew a tough word for round one: *carbuncle.* I heard the tension in her voice as she requested the definition, derivation, and alternate pronunciations. Finally, after three starts with c-a-r, she spelled, "C-a-r-b-u-n-c-l-e. *Carbuncle.*"

Lurlene was up. "Lurlene Brueggemeyer from home school. How are you, Lurlene?"

"I'm shaking like crazy. Look at my hands." She held up a trembly hand.

The audience laughed. I sucked in a smile.

"Well, I hope this isn't too painful. Your word is ER-sats. Carob was used as ersatz chocolate in the brownies. *Ersatz.*"

"*Ersatz.* E-r-s-a-t-z. *Ersatz.*" She stood there.

The pronouncer smiled. "That's correct."

"Really?" She stuck her tongue out, panting with relief. Everyone laughed again.

My word was *schuss*. How easy, I thought. I'd been skiing since I was four years old. Just to be sure I heard right, I asked for a definition.

" 'To ski directly down a slope at high speed,' " a judge read from the dictionary.

That was it. "*Schuss*. S-c-h-u-s-s. *Schuss*."

"Correct."

I took my seat. After round one, there were nineteen spellers left.

Round two took its toll. Ten people spelled out, which left only nine for round three. Kimberly was up.

"*Opossum*."

One of the classics. She shouldn't have any trouble with it.

"*Opossum*," she pronounced. "*Opossum*. May I have the definition?"

Why was she stalling? From my seat I could see that during the reading of the definition, her eyes squeezed shut. She was visualizing.

"*Opossum. Opossum.*"

Come on, Kimberly, I urged silently.

"*Opossum*. O-p . . ." The blood drained from her face. "O-p." She breathed in, then out. "O-p-p . . ."

I gasped. She'd missed it. Once you make a mistake, you can't go back and correct it. That's the rule.

Kimberly finished, "o-s-u-m. *Opposum.*"

From the judges' table, the little bell dinged. She was out.

When the pronouncer said, "Let's have a round of applause for Kimberly Tyne," I expelled softly, "Kimberly, noooo."

She must have heard me. Our eyes locked as she turned to leave the stage. Her face hardened like lava, but I knew that just beneath the crust, an eruption was about to occur.

Lurlene leaned over. "I can't believe it," she whispered.

All I could do was shake my head. I was stunned. I really expected that she and Lurlene would be the last two spellers and that whatever happened, at least one of them would win. Kimberly wanted — no, she *needed* to win. Despite what had gone on between us these last couple of months, my heart ached for her.

"Ann?" The pronouncer was staring at me. "You're up."

I jumped out of my seat.

"I thought maybe you were falling asleep on us," he said.

I smiled wanly.

"Ann, your word is NAN-uh-sek-und. *Nanosecond.* The complex mathematical equation was processed in less than a nanosecond by the computer. *Nanosecond.*"

How easy. "*Nanosecond.* N-a-n-o-s-e-c-o-n-d. *Nanosecond.*"

"Correct."

I walked back to my seat in a daze.

After round three, there were five of us left. During round four, Lurlene's word was *perambulate*. I watched her sound it out to herself, then spell it flawlessly. My word was *whippoorwill,* one I'd missed on a written test last year, which meant it was now indelibly carved into my brain.

After round four, I glanced across contestants' row. It was empty except for three chairs. Todd Myles, a seventh grader from some Catholic academy, Lurlene's, and mine. I blinked, startled by the realization that the worst I could place was third! In state!

17

The pronouncer asked us to move together in the front row. Round five began with Todd. His word was *zeppelin*. After asking for the derivation, he spelled it correctly.

Lurlene's turn. She spelled *staphylococcus* with ease. I approached the microphone. My word was *caudad*. It flashed through my mind as one of the words Kimberly and I had giggled over once. Her bogus sentence: Let's go down to the lake and catch caudads. I spelled it easily.

Round six began.

No spell-outs.

Round seven, eight, nine. Round ten and Todd was up. His word was *enfilade*.

"Could you repeat the sentence?" he asked.

"The enfilade of folding chairs in the gymnasium gave the speaker a wide aisle to walk up and down as she spoke. EN-fil-aid."

He gulped. "Derivation?"

"French," a judge said.

Todd exhaled. "*Enfilade. Enfilade.* Definition?"

The judge read it.

"Any alternate pronunciations?"

The judges conferred. "EN-fil-od," one of them said.

Todd nodded. "*Enfilade. Enfilade.* E-n-p-h-i-l-l-a-d-e. *Enphillade.*"

Lurlene and I glanced knowingly at each other. The bell dinged.

"I'm sorry," the pronouncer said. "The correct spelling is e-n-f-i-l-a-d-e. Let's have a big round of applause for Todd Myles, our third place finisher."

The audience rose to its feet. Lurlene and I applauded him as well. After he sat down in the audience, I looked at Lurlene — and panicked. We were the only ones left!

"Lurlene, Ann, please approach the microphone. As you probably know, the spell-down between the two of you will continue until one of you misses a word. If the other person spells the word correctly, along with the next one, she will be the winner. If both of you misspell the same word, the contest will continue. Do you understand?"

We nodded. Sudden death. We squeezed each other's hands.

"Lurlene, your word is *sashay*. The debutantes were instructed to sashay down the runway in prom wear. Sa-SHAY."

Lurlene looked confused. "Is there another definition? Like a sachet bag you put in your drawer to make your underwear smell good?"

The audience roared. Lurlene's face matched her dress. The pronouncer said, "No. This *sashay* means to walk or glide."

Great. We'd probably only practiced the first one, *sachet,* since it was French and had a silent letter. Double whammy.

"*Sashay*," Lurlene repeated. "S-a-s-h-a-y? *Sashay?*"

"Correct."

I breathed a sigh of relief. Good guess, my mental message went out to her as I moved in front of the microphone.

"Ann, your word is YAT-uh-gan. The Muslim's yataghan resembled a large, curved machete. *Yataghan.*"

"YAT-again?" I attempted to repeat it.

"YAT-uh-gan."

I gulped. "What's the derivation?"

The judges bent over the dictionary. "Turkish."

"Turkish?" Cripes. I couldn't have something English? "YAT-uh-gan. *Yataghan.*" Wow, the only Turkish word I knew was *afghan.* I took a stab in the dark. "Y-a-t-a-g-h-a-n." I squinched, waiting for the bell.

No bell.

"Lurlene, your word is . . ."

I backed away from the microphone.

"*Tsetse.*"

"*Tsetse,*" Lurlene repeated. "T-s-e-t-s-e. *Tsetse.*"

I've always loved that word.

"Ann, your word is *feudal.* The feudal system prevailed in England from the ninth to the thirteenth century."

I must have blacked out on the sentence. What came to mind was the homophone. "*Futile.* F-u-t-i-l-e. *Futile.*" The bell dinged.

My chin hit the mike.

"Lurlene, will you please spell *feudal?*"

She frowned at me, questioningly.

I lowered my eyes. Miss it, Lurlene. Please miss it. I couldn't believe I was thinking that.

"F-e-u-d-a-l," Lurlene spelled. "*Feudal.*"

"Correct."

Her face had apology written all over it. So did mine.

A hum began circulating in the audience. Chairs screeched across the floor as people leaned forward in their seats.

"Now, Lurlene, if you spell the next word correctly, you will become the champion. If not, Ann will have another turn. Understood?"

She nodded.

"The word is SOLL-tree. *Psaltery*. The psaltery player set the mood for the solemn ceremony. *Psaltery*."

I saw her stiffen. "SOLL-tree?" she repeated.

Come on, Lurlene, I thought. You know this word. We practiced the silent *P*'s for a week.

She mouthed the word to herself about ten times before speaking into the microphone. "SOLL-tree. Derivation?"

A judge replied, "Greek."

I sent her a mental message: Silent *P*, Lurlene.

"*Psaltery*. S-a-l-t-e-r-y. *Saltery*.

The bell dinged.

I glanced sideways at Lurlene. Her shoulders drooped.

"Ann, the word is *psaltery*."

I stepped up to the microphone. "*Psaltery*. P-s-a-l-t-r-y. *Psaltry*."

The bell dinged.

The audience moaned. I frowned. What?

One of the judges interrupted, "Actually, that is the alternate spelling, p-s-a-l-t-*r*-y, without the *e*. The speller is correct."

I heard Chase yell out, "Yeah!" while I breathed a sigh of relief.

"If you spell the next word correctly, Ann, you will become the Colorado champion and go on to represent us in the National Spelling Bee. Are you ready?"

My mouth felt like I'd been sucking chalk. I nodded.

"The word is ong-ko-ser-KY-uh-sus. *Onchocerciasis*. Onchocerciasis was discovered to be the cause of illness throughout the African village."

I knew this word. A vision of Kimberly's bedroom came back to me, along with the definition: A disease caused by filarial worms. "Please, I just ate a can of worms."

"Excuse me?" the pronouncer said.

Did I verbalize that thought? "Nothing." I blanched. "*Onchocerciasis*." I recalled every word of the discussion that night. How Mrs. Welter had assigned me to be this new girl's sponsor. Lurlene. How awful she was. How I was picked because I was soooo popular. Every word. What I couldn't recall, for the life of me, was how to spell the stupid worm word.

18

I searched the audience for Kimberly. I found her, leaning forward, elbows on knees. I closed my eyes to concentrate.

"*Onchocerciasis*," I said again. "May I have the derivation?" It wouldn't help, but I needed the time to arrange and rearrange letters in my head.

"New Latin," the judge said.

I took a deep breath. If I spelled it correctly, I won. But if I won, that meant Lurlene lost. That clunky person in red standing next to me. The person who probably got me here in the first place. She really deserved to win. I knew it. Everyone knew it.

I leaned into the microphone. "*Onchocerciasis*. O-n-c-h-o-c-e-r . . ." Suddenly I drew a blank. *K* or *C?* I wasn't sure. I'd have to guess. Shaking my head, I finished quickly: "c-i-a-s-i-s." I squinched, waiting for the bell.

No bell.

All at once I was surrounded by spellers, reporters, and people from the audience clambering to get onstage.

The next few minutes were mayhem. Reporters were flashing pictures and yelling out questions.

"How do you think you'll do at the National Spelling Bee, Ann?"

"Have you ever won anything before?"

"Did you know the last word, or were you guessing?"

I had to excuse myself. The tears were welling up in my eyes, and I didn't want anyone to see me cry. I raced for the rest room at the rear of the auditorium. At last, in the safety of a locked stall, I let the tears spill over.

God, I won! I was the Colorado state finalist. I was going to the National Spelling Bee. Me. Ann Keller. I wondered, for a fleeting moment, how my picture would look on a box of Wheaties.

It took a while to regain my composure. I blew my nose and opened the stall. She was standing there, waiting.

"Congratulations," Kimberly said, her face impassive.

"Thanks." I went to the sink to splash water on my blotchy eyes. As I was drying off with a paper towel, it suddenly struck me again. "I won. Kimberly, I won!"

She burst into tears.

"Oh, Kimberly." I reached out for her. "I'm sorry."

"No," she said, stepping back. "I'm happy for you. I am." She took off her glasses, pulled a Kleenex from her pocket, and swiped at her eyes. Sniffling, she added, "I'm glad it was you and not . . ."

She lowered her eyes at my expression. Then she said, "If you want, I'll help you prepare for nationals."

That must have been the hardest thing in the world for Kimberly to say. I opened my mouth to accept when the bathroom door swung open. "There you are!" I was suddenly engulfed in a sea of red. "Congratulations," Lurlene said. "I'm so proud of you." She took my face between her hands and squeezed — hard.

I felt Kimberly fade into the tile.

Lurlene noticed the movement behind me. "Oh, hi, Kimberly." She dropped her hands from my face. "Isn't this exciting? Now all we have to do is get her ready for Washington, D.C." Lurlene smiled into my eyes. "I just know you're going to win."

I gave a short laugh. Then I looked at Kimberly and gulped. "You still want to help?"

She hesitated.

Lurlene blurted, "She's going to need all the help she can get."

"Hey!" I whapped Lurlene's arm. Kimberly laughed. She looked at me, then at Lurlene, and back at me. Obviously it was all or nothing. Biting her lip, she nodded yes.

"Come on, then." I linked arms with my two best

friends. "We'd better get started. There's only a month before Washington and —" I stopped. "A month? To spell every word in the English language? Not to mention French and Greek and Turkish." I gulped. "How do you spell *panic?*"

Don't miss all the **SNOB SQUAD** adventures
from Julie Anne Peters:

JULIE ANNE PETERS
National Book Award Finalist

Revenge of the
SNOB SQUAD

Revenge is sweet—or is it?

JULIE ANNE PETERS
National Book Award Finalist

Romance of the
SNOB SQUAD

Romance will
never be the same!

JULIE ANNE PETERS
National Book Award Finalist

A Snitch in the
SNOB SQUAD

Will Snitching the snitch mean
the end of the Squad?

When the relay race teams are chosen in gym class, it's clear that one team doesn't have a chance of winning: Jenny is more interested in eating candy than running around a track; Prairie has a bad leg; Lydia is a complete klutz; and Max is, well, Max. But together they proudly dub themselves the Snob Squad and vow revenge on their archenemies. Let the games begin!